Homo Sapiens and Their Slow Decline Back to Cavemen

Brad Spencer

Published by Three Monkeys Books, 2026.

HOMO SAPIENS AND THEIR SLOW DECLINE BACK TO CAVEMEN

First edition. April 16, 2026.

ISBN: 979-8995690948

Written by Brad Spencer.

Table of Contents

Ex nihilo nihil fit

Nothing Comes From Nothing

DISCLAIMER
A Warning to the Easily Offended

The following text is a work of political satire. It posits a controversial theory: that the "Progressive" movement is not actually moving us forward, but is, in fact, an accidental speedrun back to the Stone Age.

While the author has gathered "evidence" by observing university campuses, Twitter (X) threads, and the organic produce aisle, this is not a peer-reviewed anthropological study. It is a comedic observation of how a specific subset of the population—primarily Democrats and modern liberals—has voluntarily abandoned survival instincts in exchange for moral superiority and government handouts.

If you are the type of person who requires a trigger warning for a book about cavemen, congratulations: You are the source material.

Chapter 1
The Fire Went Out (And the EPA Won't Let Us Relight It)

The Promethean Regret

If you rewind the clock roughly two million years—give or take a few millennia and a margin of error that would give a climate scientist a panic attack—you arrive at the single most important moment in human history. It wasn't the invention of the wheel, which was just a lazy way to avoid carrying things. It wasn't the development of agriculture, which was just a precursor to the tyranny of the HOA lawn code.

It was Fire.

Somewhere in the Great Rift Valley, a hairy, brow-heavy ancestor of ours, let's call him Grok, struck two stones together or perhaps rubbed two sticks with a vigor usually reserved for a teenager with a locked bedroom door. A spark leaped. Dry grass caught. And suddenly, the darkness retreated.

For Grok, this was everything. Fire meant warmth. Fire meant cooked meat, which allowed his brain to grow large enough to eventually invent calculus and anxiety disorders. Fire meant safety from the saber-toothed cats that were waiting in the shadows to chew on his femur. Most importantly, fire was *his*. He controlled it. He fed it. If the fire went out, Grok died. It was a simple, binary relationship with reality that kept the species sharp.

Fast forward to the present day, specifically to a studio apartment in a gentrified neighborhood of Portland or Brooklyn. Here we find the modern descendant of Grok. Let's call him skyler (lowercase intentional, because capital letters are a tool of hierarchical oppression).

Skyler is freezing.

He is wearing a beanie knitted from ethically sourced alpaca wool, a scarf that costs more than Grok's entire caloric intake for a year, and fingerless gloves that allow him to type angry threads on X (formerly Twitter) about the failures of late-stage capitalism. Skyler is cold because the power is out. The wind is not blowing, the sun is not shining, and therefore, the renewable energy grid has decided to take a mental health day.

In Grok's world, a lack of heat was a call to action. It meant finding wood, finding shelter, and exerting dominance over the environment. In Skyler's world, a lack of heat is a systemic failure of the government to provide him with a universal basic temperature.

Skyler stares at his Nest thermostat, which is currently a lifeless black circle on the wall. He taps it aggressively, as if the sheer force of his entitlement can jumpstart the electrical grid. Nothing happens. He sighs, his breath visible in the stagnant air of his eco-pod, and pulls up a podcast on his phone (battery 14%) where three people with master's degrees discuss why nuclear energy is "problematic."

This is the first step in our decline: The complete and total abdication of responsibility for our own survival.

The modern liberal does not view energy as a resource to be harvested or a force to be mastered. They view it as a magical right, something that should simply *exist*, like gravity or their parents' approval. They want the lights to turn on, the Tesla to charge, and the espresso machine to hiss, but they fundamentally oppose every efficient method of making those things happen.

They are like a caveman who wants the warmth of the fire but files a noise complaint against the crackling of the wood.

Skyler shivers. He looks at the fireplace in the corner of his pre-war apartment. It's a beautiful, brick-lined hearth that has warmed generations of Americans who actually knew how to change a tire. But Skyler cannot use it. Not because he lacks matches—though he definitely does, relying exclusively on a USB-rechargeable arc lighter that is currently dead—but because the fireplace has been sealed up.

The landlord sealed it to comply with the city's "Green New Deal" initiative, which banned wood-burning appliances to reduce particulate matter by 0.0003%. Skyler voted for this initiative. He campaigned for it. He handed out flyers printed on recycled paper that disintegrated in the rain, telling people that wood smoke was violence.

Now, as the temperature in his apartment drops below 50 degrees, Skyler is experiencing the bitter irony that usually only happens in Greek tragedies or Florida elections. He has legislated away his ability to survive.

If Grok were here, he would smash the drywall covering the fireplace with a rock, smash Skyler's reclaimed-wood coffee table into kindling, and have a roaring blaze going in ten minutes. Skyler, however, is paralyzed. Destroying the coffee table would be a waste of $400, and besides, the table is made of teak, and he isn't sure if teak emits toxins when burned. Better to freeze than to accidentally inhale a carcinogen that hasn't been FDA-approved.

He huddles deeper into his alpaca wool. He opens his phone again. The battery drops to 13%. He navigates to the website of his local utility provider to file a complaint, but the site is down. He opens Twitter to "raise awareness" of his suffering.

"Literally shaking rn," he types, his thumbs numb. "Power out for 20 mins. The city needs to do better. Vulnerable bodies are at risk. #EnergyJustice #Freezing"

He posts it. He feels a momentary rush of dopamine as a bot likes the tweet. It warms him for approximately three seconds.

This is the devolution. We have gone from *Homo erectus*, the "upright man" who conquered the night with flame, to *Homo impotens*, the "helpless man" who conquers nothing but the refresh button.

But to truly understand how we got here, we have to look at the war on the fuel itself. It wasn't enough to make the modern liberal helpless; the political elite had to make the very act of self-reliance illegal.

In the Paleolithic era, the biggest threat to maintaining a fire was a sudden rainstorm or a rival tribe stealing your coals. In the 21st century, the biggest threat is a Bureaucrat with a clipboard.

Let's imagine a scenario where Skyler actually tries to survive. Let's say the power stays out for three days. The kale is wilting in the fridge. The oat milk has turned. Desperation sets in. Skyler remembers seeing a YouTube video once about "bushcraft." He decides to go outside to the communal courtyard of his building to start a small fire to boil water (because the electric kettle is dead, and he doesn't own a pot that isn't made of ceramic-coated non-stick material that melts over an open flame).

He gathers some twigs. He piles them up. He manages, through a miracle of friction and a stolen lighter from a neighbor who actually smokes cigarettes (a Republican, obviously), to get a small flame going.

The warmth hits his face. For a split second, a genetic memory unlocks in Skyler's brain. His pupils dilate. He feels a surge of testosterone, or at least what passes for it in a body sustained by soy protein isolate. *I have made fire,* his DNA whispers. *I am man.*

"Excuse me?"

The voice cuts through the primal fog. Skyler looks up. It is not a saber-toothed tiger. It is Karen.

Karen is the final boss of modern civilization. She is the HOA president, the city council member, the HR director. She is wearing a fleece vest with a non-profit logo on it.

"You can't have an open flame here," she says, her voice possessing the nasal tone of someone who hasn't been told 'no' since 1998. "This is a smoke-free zone. Also, did you obtain a burn permit from the county? And I hope that wood isn't treated. The smoke could drift into the window of the yoga studio on the second floor."

Skyler, the temporary caveman, looks at his fire. He looks at Karen. In a sane timeline, Skyler would grunt and add more wood. But Skyler has been conditioned. He has been domesticated. The fear of breaking a rule, of being "antisocial," of being *scolded*, is stronger than his biological drive for warmth.

"I... I'm sorry," Skyler stammers. "The power is out, and..."

"We're all in this together," Karen says, which is code for *you will suffer exactly as much as I mandate.* "Put it out. Now. Or I'll have to call the non-emergency line."

Skyler stomps out his fire. He apologizes to the carbon footprint he just created. He goes back inside to freeze, secure in the knowledge that he is a good citizen.

Grok would have eaten Karen. And he would have been right to do so.

The War on Warmth

Back inside the eco-pod, the temperature has dropped another three degrees. Skyler is now wearing a second scarf. He looks like a vagrant who recently robbed a Burberry outlet.

He wanders into the kitchen, a gleaming shrine to minimalism and stainless steel. In the center of the island sits his induction cooktop. When he bought the place, the realtor—a woman named Bliss who drove a Subaru Outback covered in "Coexist" stickers—told him that induction was the future.

"It uses magnetism!" she had chirped, her eyes wide with the fervor of a religious convert. "No open flames. No methane. It's safer for the planet. Think of the polar bears, Skyler."

Skyler had thought of the polar bears. He had imagined a polar bear personally thanking him, perhaps offering him a Coca-Cola, because he chose to boil his pasta water using magnets instead of gas. So, he paid an extra $3,000 to have the existing gas line capped and the "dangerous" gas range hauled away to a landfill (where, unbeknownst to Skyler, it was immediately salvaged by a pragmatic immigrant family who are currently using it to cook a delicious, piping-hot stew while Skyler freezes).

Now, Skyler stares at the black glass surface of the induction cooktop. It is cold. It is inert. It is a very expensive paperweight.

The irony is thick enough to cut with a flint knife. The gas line is still there, right behind the wall, pressurized with sweet, combustible dinosaur ghosts. It is ready to serve. It wants to provide heat. It is a miracle of infrastructure that delivers limitless energy directly into his home for pennies. But Skyler has severed his connection to it in the name of Virtue.

He has literally cut off his nose to save the face of the planet.

This is the central neurosis of the modern Leftist relationship with energy: **The fear of density.**

Grok understood energy density. If Grok found a piece of dry hardwood, he was happy. If he found a chunk of animal fat, he was ecstatic. Fat burned hotter, longer, and brighter. Grok wanted the most bang for his buck (or the most burn for his bison).

The modern liberal, however, is terrified of efficiency. They have been conditioned to believe that if an energy source is powerful, reliable, and cheap, it must be evil.

Oil? Evil. It's black, it's sticky, and it makes trucks go vroom. Natural Gas? Sneaky evil. It burns clean, but it comes from the ground, and we shouldn't disturb Mother Gaia's internal organs. Nuclear? Scary evil. It involves atoms, and atoms are what Godzilla eats.

Instead, they worship the weak forces. They want to power a civilization of 330 million people, comprised of data centers, hospitals, and factories, using the same energy sources that Grok used to dry his loincloth: the gentle breeze and the midday sun.

Skyler moves to the window and looks out at his car parked in the driveway. It is a sleek, aerodynamic electric vehicle. We'll call it the

Voltswagon Virtue. It is currently plugged into the wall charger, which, like the rest of the house, is dead.

The car has a range of 300 miles—in ideal conditions, on a flat road, with the AC off, the radio off, and the driver holding their breath. In the current freezing temperatures, however, the battery chemistry has decided to go on strike. The range has dropped to roughly the distance one can throw a heavy rock.

Skyler realizes he can't even go sit in the car to warm up. If he turns on the car's heater, the battery will drain faster than a trust fund kid's bank account in Vegas. The car is effectively a brick. A $60,000 lithium-ion sarcophagus.

In the driveway next door, his neighbor, a man named Hank, is starting his 2004 Ford F-150. The engine roars to life. It chugs gasoline. It emits a puff of exhaust that Skyler can see from his window. Skyler instinctively recoils, his programming telling him to be offended by the emissions.

But then he sees Hank scraping the ice off the windshield, the truck's heater blasting so hard it's practically melting the glass. Hank looks warm. Hank looks mobile. Hank is not a prisoner of the grid. Hank has a tank full of liquid freedom.

Skyler feels a strange emotion. It is a mix of judgment and jealousy. He tells himself that Hank is destroying the planet. *Hank is the problem,* Skyler thinks. *Hank doesn't care about the future.*

But Hank is going to survive the night. Skyler isn't so sure.

This brings us to the "Smart Grid." The Holy Grail of the technocratic elite. The idea was to take the robust, dumb, reliable grid—which worked by simply burning stuff to make steam to spin turbines—and replace it with a "smart" system that relies on algorithms, weather patterns, and hope.

The grid failed today because the wind stopped blowing. It turns out, relying on the weather to power your society is a strategy that was abandoned in the 19th century for a reason. But we have circled back.

We have "progressed" all the way back to waiting for the rain to stop so we can get things done.

Skyler retreats to his living room. He wraps himself in a blanket made of recycled plastic bottles (which is somehow less warm than actual plastic). He realizes he needs light. The sun is setting.

He fumbles through his junk drawer. He finds a flashlight. It has no batteries because batteries are toxic. Instead, it is a "crank flashlight" he bought at an Earth Day festival.

He begins to crank it. *Whirrr-whirrr-whirrr.*

The tiny LED flickers to life, casting a sickly blue light that illuminates roughly three inches in front of him. He stops cranking. The light dies immediately.

Whirrr-whirrr-whirrr.

Skyler is now engaged in manual labor for the first time in six months. He is sweating, yet freezing. He is expending calories to generate a lumen count that a medieval peasant with a tallow candle would laugh at.

He is working harder for less result. He is the epitome of Green Energy.

Exhausted, he drops the flashlight. He sits in the dark. The silence of the apartment is oppressive. Usually, there is the hum of the refrigerator, the whir of the router, the buzz of the city. Now, there is nothing.

Just Skyler. Alone with his thoughts. And his thoughts are terrifying.

He starts to wonder if perhaps the "Preppers"—those bearded guys on YouTube who hoard beans and ammo, the ones he mocked on Reddit threads as paranoid lunatics—might have had a point. He remembers a video where a guy built a rocket stove out of cinder blocks and cooked a steak in five minutes. At the time, Skyler laughed and typed, *"Who has time for that? Just Order UberEATS, lol."*

Now, Skyler has nothing but time. And no steak.

His stomach grumbles. He realizes he hasn't eaten since his açai bowl at 10:00 AM. He navigates to his pantry by the light of his cell phone screen (8% battery remaining).

He sees jars of organic quinoa. Boxes of fair-trade pasta. A bag of artisanal coffee beans.

He realizes a horrifying truth: *None of this is food.*

Not yet. It is *potential* food. It requires processing. It requires heat. You cannot gnaw on raw pasta. You cannot crunch on dry coffee beans (well, you can, but it's a desperate move).

He looks for something ready-to-eat. He finds a box of gluten-free crackers. He eats one. It tastes like cardboard that has been vaguely introduced to the concept of salt. It provides no warmth. It provides no comfort.

He slides down to the floor, clutching the box of crackers.

In the distance, he hears the faint hum of a generator. It's coming from Hank's house. Hank has electricity. Hank probably has the game on. Hank is probably eating hot chili.

Skyler feels a tear freeze on his cheek. He hates Hank. He needs Hank.

He wonders if he should go over there. But what would he say? "Hello, oppressor. May I borrow a cup of electricity? I promise to lecture you about your privilege once I stop shivering."

No. Skyler has his pride. He will stay here, in the dark, in the cold, and wait for the government to turn the sun back on. Because that is what civilized people do.

They wait. They comply. And if they freeze, at least they freeze with a clear conscience.

The Digital Hearth and the Cold Reality

The darkness in the apartment is now absolute. Skyler's phone battery has finally surrendered, flashing a red empty icon before turning into a black mirror that reflects only his own terrified expression.

Without the blue light of the screen, Skyler feels a profound sense of amputation. He hasn't just lost communication; he has lost his external brain. He doesn't know what time it is. He doesn't know what the weather is (despite being able to feel it). He doesn't know if anyone has liked his last tweet.

In the Paleolithic era, when the fire went out, the tribe huddled together. They shared body heat. They told stories. The elders passed down wisdom about which berries would make you hallucinate and which ones would make you dead. It was a communal survival mechanism.

Skyler is alone. He has three roommates, but they are currently in their own rooms, likely undergoing similar existential crises. They do not huddle. To huddle would be an invasion of personal boundaries. To share body heat would require consent forms that cannot be printed because the printer is offline.

So, they suffer in isolation, separated by thin drywall, united only by their collective uselessness.

Skyler begins to hallucinate. Not from berries, but from withdrawal. He imagines the LED light of the router blinking. Blink. Blink. Blink. It's a phantom signal. A ghost of connectivity.

He realizes, with a shudder that has nothing to do with the cold, that he has no survival skills. None. He has a Master's degree in Critical Theory of 19th Century Interpretive Dance, but he cannot boil water without an app. He can deconstruct a narrative, but he cannot construct a shelter. He can identify a micro-aggression from fifty yards away, but he cannot identify the cardinal direction of "North."

He is the apex of evolution, stripped of his pedestal. He is a naked ape who forgot he was an ape.

And then, he has a thought. A dangerous, radical thought.

I should burn something.

It is the spirit of Grok, clawing its way through layers of soy and social conditioning. Skyler looks around the room. He needs fuel.

He looks at his bookshelf. It is filled with pristine hardcovers he has never read but displays prominently to signal his intelligence to guests. Capital in the Twenty-First Century. The Uninhabitable Earth. How to Be an Antiracist.

They are made of paper. Paper burns.

He reaches for a book. His hand trembles. To burn a book is the ultimate taboo. It is what the "bad guys" do in history. But his fingers are turning blue. Logic dictates that survival supersedes symbolism.

He grabs a copy of a dense political manifesto. He opens it. The pages are dry. It would burn beautifully. He reaches for his dead lighter, remembering he has a box of decorative matches in the bathroom—matches he bought because the box had a picture of a cat on it.

He fumbles in the dark, finds the matches, and strikes one. The smell of sulfur—the scent of hell, or salvation—fills the air. The flame flares up, yellow and hot.

He brings the flame to the corner of the page.

Stop.

His conscience intervenes. If you burn this book, the voice in his head says, you are betraying the cause. You are destroying knowledge. You are no better than the barbarians.

Skyler hesitates. The match burns down. It reaches his fingertips. He yelps and drops it. The match goes out. The book remains unburnt.

He sighs. He cannot do it. He would rather freeze to death as an intellectual martyr than survive as a pragmatic book-burner. He puts the book back on the shelf.

"At least I kept my principles," he whispers to the empty room.

Ten minutes later, the lights flicker.

A collective gasp echoes through the apartment building. The hum returns. The refrigerator kicks on with a shudder. The router's LEDs turn from angry red to hopeful amber, and finally, to glorious, steady green.

The grid is back.

Skyler leaps to his feet. He doesn't run to the heater. He runs to the wall outlet. He plugs in his phone.

As the screen lights up, the dopamine hits his brain like a freight train. He is connected. He is safe. He is online.

The heat begins to flow from the vents. The induction stove beeps. The smart speaker announces, "I am connected to the internet."

Skyler does not drop to his knees to thank the line workers who presumably just battled ice and wind to repair a transformer. He does not vow to buy a generator, or a gas stove, or even a warm coat. He does not reflect on his fragility.

Instead, he opens Twitter.

He sees that the power outage was trending. He sees that thousands of others were also cold. He feels validated. He types a new update:

"Power back on. Honestly, surviving that was traumatic. It really shows how our infrastructure fails the most marginalized among us. We need a federal inquiry. Also, does anyone know if the vegan Thai place is delivering yet?"

He hits send. He orders food. He sits back on his couch, the ordeal already fading into the realm of "content."

He has learned nothing.

Somewhere, buried deep in his DNA, Grok weeps. Grok knows that the fire will go out again. And next time, it might stay out.

Skyler, however, is busy scrolling. He has moved on. The cave is warm again, the shadows have retreated, and the glowing rectangle is telling him everything is fine.

But the decline is real. Skyler has survived not because he is strong, but because the system that cradles him is resilient. He is a passenger in his own life, a pet kept by a machine he does not understand.

And as he scrolls, his language begins to deteriorate. He isn't writing essays. He isn't telling stories. He is typing "FR" (For Real) and "NB" (Not Bad) and posting a GIF of a raccoon eating a grape.

The fire is back, but the mind is dimming.

Which brings us to the next step in our regression. We have lost the mastery of the elements. Now, we must examine the loss of the very thing that separates us from the beasts: The ability to speak clearly.

Skyler puts down his phone and yells to his roommate:

"Yooo! Food's here!"

"Bet," the roommate replies.

Two million years of linguistic evolution, reduced to two syllables.

Welcome to the New Stone Age.

Chapter 2
Grunts, Groans, and Pronouns

The Tower of Babble

Language is the crown jewel of humanity. It is the tool that allows us to coordinate hunts, draft the Magna Carta, and explain to a waiter exactly how we want our eggs poached. It took millions of years for our larynxes to drop and our brains to expand enough to turn guttural noises into sonnets. We moved from pointing and grunting to the eloquence of Cicero and the wit of Twain.

And then, somewhere around 2015, we decided we'd had enough of clarity.

If you walk through a modern university campus or scroll through the Slack channel of a progressive tech startup, you will witness a linguistic phenomenon that baffles anthropologists. It is not an evolution; it is a retreat. We are witnessing the birth of *Homo Offensus*—a creature so terrified of saying the wrong thing that they have effectively stopped saying anything at all.

In the Paleolithic era, communication was high-stakes but simple. Caveman A: *"Tiger behind rock."* Caveman B: *"Run."*

The message was clear. The data was actionable. The survival rate was high. If Caveman A had been a modern liberal, the conversation would have gone something like this:

Caveman A: "I want to hold space for the possibility that there may be a non-human entity of feline descent situated behind that geological formation, but I don't want to assign aggressive intent to it because that reinforces predator stereotypes." Caveman B: [Gets eaten while waiting for the sentence to end.]

We have replaced directness with a linguistic fog so dense you need a machete to hack through it. This is not about politeness; it is about fear. The modern liberal speaks not to communicate truth, but to navigate a minefield where the mines are constantly being moved by teenagers on TikTok.

Let's return to our protagonist, Skyler.

Skyler is sitting in a coffee shop called "The Daily Grind" (ironic, because no one inside looks like they do manual labor). He is meeting with his friend, River. River is a non-binary, post-structuralist poet who is currently working on a master's thesis about the colonial implications of oatmeal.

Skyler wants to tell River that River has a piece of spinach in their teeth.

In a sane world—say, 1995—Skyler would say: *"Hey, you got something in your teeth."* River would pick it out. Life would go on.

But this is the 2020s. Skyler freezes. His internal processor begins to overheat. He runs a diagnostic check on his potential sentence:

1. Is pointing out a flaw in appearance body shaming? 2. Is spinach a cultural food that I, as a white male, have no right to comment on? 3. Does the phrase "in your teeth" imply that teeth are the standard, thereby marginalizing the dentally challenged? 4. If I speak, am I taking up space that should be reserved for marginalized voices?

Skyler sweats. He stares at the spinach. It is a leafy green flag of defiance waving against the enamel.

"Is something wrong?" River asks, sensing Skyler's intense gaze.

"No!" Skyler blurts out. "I mean, yes. I mean... I just... I want to acknowledge your presence and validate your choices."

"Thank you," River says, sipping their matcha latte. The spinach remains.

Skyler has failed. The simple act of communication—transferring a fact from Brain A to Brain B—was short-circuited by the fear of offense. He decides it is safer to let River walk around with vegetable matter in their mouth than to risk a micro-aggression.

This is the new grunt. It isn't a lack of words; it's a deluge of words that mean nothing. We use "corporate speak" and "academic jargon" as a shield. We say "we are pivoting to a synergy-based holistic approach" when we mean "we are firing Dave." We say "unhoused neighbors experiencing temporary displacement" when we mean "the homeless guy screaming at a pigeon."

We have become terrified of reality. And when you fear reality, you fear the words that describe it.

Consider the obsession with changing definitions. In the cave, a rock was a rock. You couldn't argue that the rock was actually a cloud because the rock would hit you in the head and prove its rock-ness. But in the modern liberal bubble, definitions are fluid. They are soft. They are Play-Doh.

Recession? No, that's just "negative growth transition." Riot? No, that's a "mostly peaceful fiery gathering." Illegal Alien? No, that's an "undocumented dreamer with unauthorized entry status."

By softening the language, we soften our brains. We lose the ability to grapple with hard truths. We become like children who cover their ears and hum so they don't have to hear that bedtime is in five minutes.

Skyler and River eventually leave the coffee shop. They walk past a construction site. Here, the linguistic divide is stark.

The construction workers—men with calloused hands and sunburned necks—are shouting. *"Hey! Watch out! Crane coming through!" "Grab that sheet!" "Move your ass!"*

Skyler flinches. The language is rough. It is abrasive. It lacks nuance.

But guess what? The building is getting built. The steel is going up. The concrete is pouring. These men are operating in the physical world, where gravity doesn't care about your feelings and a falling I-beam won't pause to ask for your pronouns.

Skyler looks at them with a mix of disdain and fear. He views their directness as "toxic masculinity." He believes their shouting is a sign of low intelligence.

He is wrong. Their shouting is a sign of high survival instinct. They are the hunters coordinating the kill. Skyler is the gatherer wandering into a ravine because he was too polite to ask for directions.

As Skyler walks away, he pulls out his phone to tweet about the "aggressive energy" of the construction site. He types:

"Just walked past a construction zone. The energy was so hostile. Why is toxic masculinity so loud? We need to reimagine labor as a silent, meditative practice."

He stares at the tweet. He deletes "masculinity" and replaces it with "patriarchal expression" just to be safe. He hits send.

He feels good. He has contributed to the discourse. He has signaled his virtue.

Meanwhile, back at the site, a worker named Tony yells, "Lunch!"

And everyone understands him perfectly.

The Ritual of the Circle

Later that evening, Skyler attends a gathering. It is not a "party," because parties imply hedonism and lack of structure. It is a "Community Synergy Mixer" held in the basement of a local co-op. The goal is to organize a protest against a new bakery that didn't put a rainbow sticker in their window during Pride Month.

Skyler enters the room. In a primitive tribe, entering a new space involved assessing threats: *Who is the strongest? Where is the exit? Is that meat fresh?*

In the modern liberal tribe, the assessment is entirely linguistic. What are the current rules? What words have been banned since this morning?

The facilitator, a person named Ash who is wearing a jumpsuit that looks like it was made from oat sacks, claps their hands.

"Okay everyone! Let's circle up! We're going to do introductions. Name, pronouns, and—just to ground us—your favorite non-appropriative comfort food."

Skyler's heart rate spikes to 140 bpm. This is the modern equivalent of a saber-toothed tiger jumping out of a bush. It is the "Circle of Doom."

The circle begins.

"I'm Kai," says the first person. "They/Them. I like toast." "I'm Wren," says the next. "She/They. But on Tuesdays, I prefer He/Him, unless it's raining. I like hummus."

Skyler's brain is sprinting. He is fourth in line. He has to memorize Wren's weather-dependent gender identity while simultaneously calculating his own. He is a cis-gendered white male. In this room, that is a social credit score of negative one thousand. He needs to sound apologetic about his existence.

"I'm Skyler," he stammers when his turn comes. "He/Him... but I'm open to learning? And I like... potatoes? But not, like, *Irish Famine* potatoes. Just... general tubers."

He exhales. He survived. But the mental energy expended in those ten seconds could have been used to track a deer for three miles.

This is the Cognitive Load Theory of De-evolution.

The human brain consumes about 20% of the body's energy. In the past, that energy was used for spatial reasoning, tool making, and situational awareness. Today, the modern liberal burns those calories navigating a labyrinth of identity politics.

They are exhausted not because they have worked hard, but because they are running a constant background simulation of *How Not To Get Cancelled.*

After the introductions, the group breaks out into conversation. Skyler finds himself talking to a woman named Luna. The conversation turns to the bakery they are planning to protest.

"I just think it's important we hit them where it hurts," Skyler says, trying to sound militant. "We need to kill two birds with one stone."

The room goes silent. The air leaves the basement.

Luna looks at Skyler with eyes wide with horror. "Skyler," she whispers. "The language."

"What?" Skyler panics. "The bakery?"

"No," Ash interjects, gliding over like a referee at a soccer match. "You said 'kill two birds.' That is violent, speciesist language. We don't use idioms that normalize animal cruelty."

Skyler blinks. "I... I didn't mean actual birds."

"Intent doesn't matter," Ash recites, the mantra of the tribe. "Impact matters. Your words created an unsafe environment for the avian-identified."

"The correct phrase," Luna says gently, "is 'Feed two birds with one scone.'"

Skyler feels his soul leave his body. He nods. "Right. Feed two birds. With a scone. I'm sorry. I'm unlearning."

"Thank you for doing the work," Ash says, and the tension dissipates.

Let's pause and look at this from an evolutionary standpoint.

Language is supposed to be efficient. "Kill two birds with one stone" conveys a complex idea: Efficiency in action. It is visceral. It makes sense to a hunter. "Feed two birds with one scone" conveys... what? That we are bird feeders? That we have surplus baked goods? It is soft. It is toothless.

But more importantly, it is a **trap**.

The rules of this language change so fast that no one can actually master them. This is a feature, not a bug. In a tribe where everyone is competing for moral status, the ability to correct someone's grammar is a power move. It is the new club to the head.

If Grok wanted to dominate a rival, he hit him with a rock. If Ash wants to dominate Skyler, Ash corrects his idiom. The result is the same: Submission.

Skyler spends the rest of the mixer in a state of terrified silence. He nods. He smiles. He hums in agreement. But he does not speak, because speaking is dangerous.

He has become a mime in his own life.

This is the ultimate irony of the "Communication Age." We have more ways to talk than ever before—text, tweet, DM, Zoom—but we are saying less and less. We are reverting to a pre-linguistic state where safety is found in silence.

As the meeting wraps up, Skyler walks out into the cool night air. He sees a homeless man asking for change. The man is not worried about pronouns. The man is not worried about speciesist idioms.

"Hey buddy," the man says. "Got a dollar?"

It is a refreshing blast of reality. A clear question. A direct request.

Skyler fumbles in his pocket. He doesn't have cash; he only has Apple Pay.

"I... I don't have cash," Skyler says. "But I see you. I validate your struggle."

The homeless man looks at him. "I can't eat validation, man."

The man turns away, disgusted. He has identified Skyler as a useless member of the species. A gatherer with nothing to gather. A hunter with no spear.

Skyler walks home, his head buzzing with the new rules he has to memorize. Feed two birds with one scone. Don't assume genders. Silence is violence, but speech is also violence.

He is mentally exhausted. He yearns for a simpler time. A time he never knew. A time when a grunt meant "hungry" and a scream meant "run," and nobody stopped to ask the tiger if it preferred to be called a "feline person of size."

But that time is gone. Skyler is trapped in the Tower of Babble, and he is adding bricks to his own prison, one corrected sentence at a time.

The Witness Who Saw Nothing (Politically Speaking)

Skyler arrives back at his apartment complex just in time to witness a crime.

It is a classic modern crime: The Porch Piracy.

A figure is standing on the stoop, holding a box that had been delivered earlier that day. The box contains Skyler's new artisan-crafted, fair-trade, conflict-free beard oil (Skyler cannot grow a beard, but he is manifesting one).

The thief looks directly at Skyler. Skyler looks directly at the thief.

In the Paleolithic era, this interaction would have been brief and violent. Grok sees thief taking meat. Grok throws rock. Grok gets meat back. Justice is served. No paperwork required.

But Skyler is not Grok. Skyler is a member of the *Homo Offensus*. His first instinct is not to defend his property—because property is theft, according to the book he almost burned earlier—but to analyze the *socio-economic factors* that led to this moment.

The thief, realizing Skyler is not going to charge at him with a spear, casually walks to a waiting bicycle and pedals away.

Skyler fumbles for his phone. He dials 911. This is a moral compromise for Skyler, who frequently tweets "Defund the Police," but he really wants that beard oil.

"911, what is your emergency?" a tired voice answers.

"Hi," Skyler whispers, hiding behind a recycling bin. "I just witnessed a... a non-consensual transfer of property."

"A theft?" the dispatcher asks. "Did you see who did it?"

"Yes," Skyler says. "They just left."

"Okay, sir. I need a description. Male or female?"

Skyler freezes. The trap has sprung.

He saw the thief. The thief had a beard, broad shoulders, and was wearing a t-shirt that said *FBI: Female Body Inspector*. By any biological metric available to the human eye for the last 200,000 years, the thief was a man.

But Skyler cannot say that. To assume gender is violence.

"I... I couldn't possibly ascertain their gender identity from a distance," Skyler says, his voice trembling with righteousness. "They presented in a way that aligns with traditional patriarchal aesthetics, but they could be non-binary or gender-fluid."

There is a long pause on the line. "Okay," the dispatcher sighs. "Was the suspect white, black, Hispanic, Asian?"

Skyler breaks into a cold sweat. This is the ultimate minefield. If he mentions race, he is engaging in profiling. He is perpetuating the carceral state. He is part of the pipeline.

"Race is a social construct," Skyler lectures the emergency operator. "To assign a racial category to this individual would be to participate in a system of oppression that dates back to colonialization. Also, it was dark."

"Sir," the dispatcher says, losing patience. "What color was their skin?"

"It was... melanin-enriched? But also, maybe they had a tan? I don't want to center my whiteness by making assumptions about their ethnic background."

"Okay," the dispatcher says, the sound of aggressive typing audible in the background. "Let's try this. What were they wearing?"

"A shirt," Skyler offers. "And pants."

"What color shirt?"

"Blue. But," Skyler adds quickly, "it looked like a mass-produced textile, likely fast fashion. This suggests the individual is a victim of late-stage capitalism and probably stealing out of necessity. Really, *I* am the villain here for hoarding resources."

"Sir, did they take your package?"

"Yes."

"And you can't tell me if it was a man or a woman, white or black, tall or short?"

"Height is ableist," Skyler mutters. "And describing weight is fat-phobic."

"So you saw a shapeless, colorless, genderless entity impacted by capitalism take your box?"

"Yes," Skyler says. "Exactly."

"We'll send a patrol car to... look around," the dispatcher lies. "Have a nice night."

The line goes dead.

Skyler stands up, brushing dirt off his knees. He has lost his beard oil. He has lost his dignity. But he has kept his vocabulary pure. He has refused to use the "oppressive" tools of description. He has successfully communicated *nothing*.

As he walks up to his door, he sees a note left by the thief. It's written on the back of a pizza flyer. It says:

THANKS FOR THE OIL, BRO. NICE BEANIE.

The thief used gendered language ("Bro"). The thief used direct language ("Thanks"). The thief is winning.

Skyler goes inside and locks the door. He sits on his couch and opens his laptop. He needs to process this trauma. He navigates to his blog, *The Daily Deconstruction*.

He begins to type a new post titled: Why My Robbery Was Actually an Act of Restorative Justice.

He types: Today, I experienced a redistribution of assets. While my initial reaction was fear—a byproduct of my conditioned privilege—I realized that the person who took my package needed it more than I did. Language failed me, but empathy prevailed.

He deletes "Language failed me." He replaces it with: *Language evolved.*

He posts it. No one comments.

This is the end of the line for human communication. We started with grunts that meant everything. We evolved to Shakespearean sonnets that explored the human soul. And now, we have arrived at the "Thread." A collection of words so sanitized, so filtered, and so terrified of reality that they evaporate upon contact with the air.

In the cave, if you couldn't describe the tiger, the tiger ate you. In the modern city, if you can't describe the criminal, the criminal takes your stuff and laughs at you.

We are slowly becoming a species of mutes, gesturing wildly at problems we are not allowed to name. We are the architects of our own confusion, building a Tower of Babel out of pronouns and euphemisms, waiting for it to collapse.

And when it does, when the words finally fail completely, we will be left with only the old tools. The tools that don't need words.

The rock. The fire. The spear.

But Skyler doesn't know how to use any of those. So he just refreshes his browser, waiting for a "Like" to tell him he still exists.

Chapter 3
The Gatherers (Who Can't Hunt)

The Apex Predator of Aisle 4

Biologically speaking, the human being is a masterpiece of violence. We have forward-facing eyes for tracking prey. We have shoulders evolved for throwing spears. We have a digestive system capable of processing almost anything, and teeth designed to tear through muscle and gristle. We are, by design, the Apex Predator of the planet. When a lion sees a human, it doesn't see a snack; it sees a problem.

Or at least, it used to.

If a lion were to see Skyler walking down the street today, clutching a reusable tote bag that says *"Kale is the New Beef,"* the lion would not feel fear. It would feel confusion. It might even feel pity.

Skyler is currently engaged in the modern equivalent of the Great Hunt. He is at *Gaia's Bounty*, a high-end organic grocery store where the produce is misted with filtered spring water and the prices are high enough to induce a mild stroke.

Skyler is hungry. In the Paleolithic era, hunger was a simple equation: *Find animal. Kill animal. Eat animal.* It was high-risk, high-reward.

For Skyler, hunger is a high-stress negotiation with ethical labels.

He is currently stalking a carton of eggs. He stands in front of the refrigerated case, paralyzed by the paradox of choice. There are twelve different brands of eggs, each promising a higher level of chicken happiness than the last.

- **Brand A:** Cage-Free. (Sounds good, but what if the "cage" is just a crowded room?)

- **Brand B:** Free-Range. (Better, but how big is the range?)
- **Brand C:** Pasture-Raised. (Okay, so they saw grass.)
- **Brand D:** "Heritage Breed, Soy-Free, Regeneratively Farmed, forest-bathed chickens named by a therapist."

Skyler picks up Brand D. A dozen eggs cost $14.50. He grimaces. That is expensive. But if he buys the $4.00 eggs, he is essentially funding a chicken concentration camp. He imagines a sad chicken looking at him with judgmental eyes.

He puts the $14.50 eggs in his cart. He has successfully hunted protein, but he feels no triumph. He feels only financial guilt and moral exhaustion.

He moves to the meat department. This is the most dangerous territory for the modern liberal. Skyler eats meat, but he treats it like a shameful secret, like a nicotine addiction or a subscription to a non-woke comedian's podcast.

He stares at the beef.

Grok, his ancestor, knew exactly what beef was. It was the inside of a bison. It was warm, bloody, and difficult to obtain. Grok respected the animal because the animal had tried to kill him first.

Skyler wants the beef to look as little like an animal as possible. He recoils at the sight of a "Tomahawk Ribeye" because the bone is sticking out. The bone reminds him that this was a living creature with a skeleton. It is too visceral. It is too... *real.*

He prefers the ground beef. It is a pink, amorphous sludge in a Styrofoam tray. It has no face. It has no anatomy. It is an abstraction of meat. It allows him to dissociate the burger from the cow.

He picks up a package of "Grass-Fed, 90% Lean Ground Sirloin." He scans the QR code on the package to read the biography of the rancher. The website assures him that the cows were read poetry before slaughter. Skyler feels better.

But then, disaster strikes.

He turns the corner and bumps into a display of whole fish.

Skyler freezes. The fish have heads. They have eyes. And the eyes are looking at him.

In a survival situation, a fish is a miracle. It is a packet of protein and fat that can keep you alive for days. You smash it with a rock, gut it with a sharp stone, and roast it over a fire.

Skyler, however, feels a wave of nausea. "Ew," he whispers.

He cannot handle the reality of the food chain. He wants the filet. He wants the square block of white protein that comes in a vacuum-sealed bag. He wants the sanitized, industrial output of the very system he claims to hate.

He bypasses the fish and heads for the "Plant-Based Alternatives" section.

Here, Skyler feels safe. He picks up a package of "Beyond Mystery Sludge." The ingredients list is longer than the Magna Carta. It contains methylcellulose, potato starch, sunflower lecithin, and beet juice extract for "coloring."

It is a chemical experiment molded into the shape of a patty. It is processed food, the very thing health experts warn against. But it makes Skyler feel virtuous. He isn't eating an animal; he is eating a science project.

He throws it in the cart.

As he navigates the aisles, Skyler is technically "gathering." But unlike the gatherers of old, who knew which berries would cure a headache and which would stop your heart, Skyler knows nothing about the botanical nature of his food.

He buys a bag of "Superfood Salad Mix." It contains kale, chard, and something called "mizuna." Skyler doesn't know what Mizuna is. If he saw it growing in a crack in the sidewalk, he would spray it with Round-Up (or rather, an organic vinegar solution). But because it is in a plastic clamshell box with a picture of a smiling farmer, he assumes it is vital for his survival.

He is foraging by branding.

He reaches the checkout. He does not carry his kill home on his back. He does not drag it through the snow. He places his reusable bag on the counter.

The cashier, a young woman with a nose ring and a t-shirt that says *Eat the Rich*, scans his items.

"Did you find everything okay?" she asks.

"Yes," Skyler says. "But the layout is a bit aggressive today. The butchery section is really... present."

"I know," she sighs. "I'm trying to get management to put up a trigger warning for the seafood display. The eyes are a lot."

"Totally," Skyler agrees.

He pays with his phone. He walks out to his car. He has successfully obtained calories without expending any. He has gathered food without knowing where it came from, how it grew, or how it died.

He is the most well-fed, malnourished creature in history. He has a cart full of "nutrient-dense" foods, but if you dropped him in a forest with a knife and a fishing line, he would starve to death within a week, likely while trying to Google "is this moss gluten-free?"

As he loads his car, he sees a bumper sticker on a pickup truck parked next to him. It depicts a deer silhouette and the words *Meat is Meat.*

Skyler sneers. "Barbarian," he thinks.

Then he drives home to cook his fake meat on his electric stove, completely unaware that he is the one who has forgotten how to be human.

The Digital Safari

Back in his kitchen, Skyler attempts to prepare the "Beyond Mystery Sludge."

In the wild, cooking is a chemical reaction controlled by intuition. You watch the fat render, you smell the char, you feel the heat. It is a dance with physics.

Skyler, however, treats cooking like he treats a political debate: He tries to force the outcome through sheer willpower and rigid adherence to a script. The package says, "Cook on Medium-High for 4 minutes." Skyler turns the knob to exactly 7. He sets a timer on his phone. He stands back, arms crossed, expecting the laws of thermodynamics to obey the instructions on the cardboard box.

They do not.

Because Skyler is using a non-stick pan that has lost its coating (he scrubbed it with steel wool, unaware that Teflon is not invincible), the sludge immediately fuses to the metal. Smoke begins to rise. It is not the savory smoke of a campfire; it is the acrid, chemical smoke of burning pea protein and binding agents.

The smoke alarm goes off.

BEEP! BEEP! BEEP!

This is the call of the modern wild. It is the signal that the Gatherer has failed.

Skyler waves a tea towel at the alarm, screaming, "I'm just trying to nourish myself!"

He scrapes the blackened, yet somehow still frozen, patty into the compost bin. He is defeated. The expensive grocery run was a failure. He has gathered the ingredients, but he lacks the fire-mastery to transform them into sustenance.

He is starving. The primal brain takes over. He needs calories. Now.

He reaches for his spear.

By which I mean, he unlocks his iPhone 16 and opens **UberEATS**.

This is the new Savannah. The interface is lush with colorful images of prey: Sushi, Tacos, Burgers, Pad Thai. Skyler is no longer a failed cook; he is a Master Hunter surveying his domain.

He scrolls. He is looking for the perfect kill. It must meet his strict criteria:

1. **Rating:** Must be above 4.8 stars. (He will not risk his digestion on a 4.5 star gazelle.)
2. **Distance:** Must be close enough to arrive warm, but far enough that he feels he is accessing "exotic" cuisine (i.e., the other side of the river).
3. **Vibe:** The restaurant must have a name like "The Rustic Spoon" or "Farm & Fable."

He spots his target: A place called *Harvest Bowl.* They sell bowls of grain and leaves for $22. It is exactly the kind of inefficient caloric return Skyler loves.

He taps "Order."

Now begins the **Tracking Phase**.

In the Pleistocene, tracking a wounded mammoth took days. You had to read broken twigs, disturbed grass, and the scent of fear on the wind. It required total sensory immersion.

Skyler tracks his dinner via a blue line on a Google Map.

"Your Dasher, Brayden, is at the restaurant," the app informs him.

Skyler stares at the screen, mesmerized. The little car icon moves. *Brayden has the food.* The prey has been secured. Now, the transport begins.

Skyler watches the little car navigate traffic. He feels a surge of anxiety when the car stops at a red light for too long. *Why has he stopped?* Skyler thinks, his hunter's instinct flaring. *Has a rival tribe intercepted the grain bowl? Is Brayden eating my quinoa?*

This is the ultimate disconnect. Skyler is technically "hunting," but he has outsourced the danger. Brayden is the one battling the elements. Brayden is the one dodging the potholes and the road-raging BMWs. Brayden is the proxy hunter, risking his life in a 2008 Honda Civic so Skyler can remain safe in his temperature-controlled pod.

Skyler does not think about Brayden. He does not wonder if Brayden has health insurance. He does not wonder if the tip he entered ($2.00, because "service fees are theft") is sufficient. He views Brayden as a biological drone, a mechanism for calorie delivery.

The little car icon turns onto Skyler's street. The excitement peaks. The kill is imminent.

Skyler paces by the door. He does not want to interact with the provider. That would break the illusion. If he sees Brayden, he has to acknowledge that a human being just brought him food like a servant. That feels icky.

He selected the "Leave at Door" option. The modern liberal loves humanity in the abstract, but prefers "Contactless Delivery" in the specific.

His phone buzzes. *"Delivered."*

Skyler counts to ten. He waits for the sound of retreating footsteps. He cracks the door open.

There, on the welcome mat, sits the brown paper bag. The spoil of war.

He grabs it and retreats into his cave. He unpacks the *Harvest Bowl.* It is lukewarm. The dressing has leaked slightly. But to Skyler, it is a triumph.

He sits on his couch, fork in hand. He takes a bite of the kale and ancient grains. He feels satisfied. He has survived another day. He has conquered the app.

But let us compare this to the actual hunter.

When a hunter kills a deer, he feels a complex mix of adrenaline, gratitude, and solemnity. He knows exactly where the meat came from. He knows the cost of life. He processes the animal with his own hands. Every bite connects him to the earth.

Skyler connects to nothing. He eats his bowl while watching a Netflix documentary about how industrial farming is bad, completely oblivious to the fact that his $22 grain bowl was grown on an industrial farm, packaged in industrial plastic, and delivered by the gig-economy equivalent of a serf.

He finishes the bowl. He is still hungry. The grains were not dense enough.

He goes back to the kitchen. He opens the pantry. He sees a bag of flour.

I could make bread, he thinks. Everyone made bread during the pandemic. It's primal. It's natural.

He Googles "How to make sourdough starter."

Step 1: Capture wild yeast from the air.

Skyler looks at the air in his apartment. It is filtered through a HEPA purifier. It smells of essential oils and stagnation. There is no wild yeast here. There is no "wild" anything here.

He closes the tab. He realizes he cannot make bread. He can only buy bread.

He is a Gatherer with no basket, a Hunter with no spear. He is entirely, utterly dependent on the System to keep him alive.

If the app servers went down tomorrow, Skyler would be looking at that bag of flour and wondering if he could snort it.

And thus, the decline continues. We have traded the ability to feed ourselves for the convenience of having someone else do it for us, while we sit on the couch and critique their driving.

But the saddest part is yet to come. Because Skyler, in his quest to reconnect with nature, is about to try something even more foolish than UberEats.

He is going to try **Urban Foraging**.

The Call of the Wild (Dandelion)

It is Saturday morning. The sun is shining. Skyler has decided that today is the day he breaks the chains of the industrial food complex once and for all. He is done with the grocery store. He is done with the delivery apps.

He is going Urban Foraging.

He read an article on *Vice* about a woman in Brooklyn who makes her own pesto from weeds she finds in sidewalk cracks. It seemed revolutionary. It seemed sticking-it-to-the-man. It seemed like free food.

Skyler prepares for his expedition. He puts on his "technical hiking pants" (which have never hiked further than a brunch line). He grabs a wicker basket he bought for $65 at a vintage market. He downloads an app called *PlantIdentify: Nature in Your Pocket*.

He steps out into the urban jungle.

In the Paleolithic era, a Gatherer was a master botanist. A Gatherer knew the difference between a mushroom that would give you dinner and a mushroom that would give you a conversation with God followed by liver failure. This knowledge was hard-won, passed down through oral tradition and the occasional tragic funeral.

Skyler has no oral tradition. He has an algorithm.

He walks to the local city park. To the uninitiated, this is just a patch of grass where teenagers vape and Golden Retrievers do their business. To Skyler, this is the Garden of Eden.

He spots a patch of green leafy things near a park bench. His heart races.

Is that... wild arugula?

He crouches down. He pulls out his phone. He snaps a photo of the weed. The app thinks for a moment, spinning its digital wheel.

Result: 62% Match: Dandelion Greens (Taraxacum officinale). **Secondary Result:** 38% Match: Common Ragweed (Ambrosia artemisiifolia).

Skyler ignores the 38%. He is an optimist. He manifests the dandelion. He read that dandelions are a "superfood," packed with vitamins and antioxidants, and more importantly, they are anti-establishment. They grow where they aren't wanted. Skyler resonates with this energy.

He pulls a handful of the leaves from the ground. He shakes off a little bit of dirt.

Look at me, he thinks. I am providing.

He brings a leaf to his nose. It smells earthy. It smells like the soil of Mother Gaia. (It also smells faintly of ammonia, but Skyler attributes this to the "mineral richness" of the park soil).

He takes a bite.

It is bitter. Violently bitter. It tastes like a battery wrapped in spinach.

Grok, his ancestor, would have tasted this, spat it out, and moved on to find a berry. Bitterness in nature is often a warning sign: *Do not eat me, I am poison.*

But Skyler has been conditioned by the modern wellness industry to believe that if something tastes bad, it must be "detoxifying." Kale tastes like punishment, and Kale is good for you. Therefore, this sidewalk weed must be the elixir of life.

He swallows. He feels a surge of pride. He puts the rest of the handful in his $65 basket.

"Hey! What are you doing?"

Skyler looks up. A man in a neon yellow vest is approaching. He is pushing a lawnmower. He is a member of the Parks and Recreation maintenance crew. Let's call him Mike.

Mike is not a Gatherer. Mike is a man who just wants to finish mowing the lawn before lunch.

"I'm foraging," Skyler says, beaming. "Just harvesting some local greens. Reconnecting with the land, you know?"

Mike looks at the basket. He looks at the patch of weeds Skyler just pulled from. He looks back at Skyler.

"Buddy," Mike says, leaning on the handle of his mower. "I wouldn't eat those."

"Why?" Skyler asks, his tone defensive. "Is it because of city ordinances? I believe the earth belongs to everyone."

"No," Mike says. "It's because I sprayed that whole patch with Roundup on Tuesday. Also, that's exactly where the homeless guy, 'Screaming Jimmy,' pees every morning at 6:00 AM."

Skyler freezes.

The "earthy" taste in his mouth suddenly takes on a new, horrifying context. The ammonia smell creates a vivid mental picture.

The chemical warfare of the Roundup battles the biological warfare of Screaming Jimmy in Skyler's stomach.

"Roundup?" Skyler whispers. "But... that's a carcinogen."

"Yeah, well, it kills the weeds," Mike says, starting his mower. "Good luck with the detox."

Mike walks away. Skyler is left alone with his basket of poison-pee-weeds.

Panic sets in.

In the wild, if you ate a poison berry, you induced vomiting or you chewed on charcoal. You took immediate physical action.

Skyler takes digital action. He drops the basket. He pulls out his phone. He opens WebMD.

He types: Ingested herbicide and human urine symptoms.

The internet, being a helpful place, immediately tells him that he has cancer, kidney failure, and possibly rabies. It suggests he is already dead.

Skyler begins to hyperventilate. He is having a psychosomatic reaction. His throat feels tight (it's just anxiety). His stomach churns (it's just the realization that he ate pee).

He dials his doctor's office. It goes to voicemail. It is Saturday.

He considers calling 911, but the shame holds him back. How can he explain to the dispatcher—the same one who took his call about the gender-neutral porch pirate—that he voluntarily ate a weed in a public park because a blog told him it was empowering?

He stumbles to a nearby water fountain. He rinses his mouth out for five minutes. He looks at his reflection in a puddle.

He sees a man who has dual master's degrees. He sees a man who understands the nuances of geopolitical conflicts. He sees a man who can code in Python.

And he sees a man who just ate a urinal cake made of vegetation because he forgot that Nature is not a theme park.

He leaves the basket. He walks home.

On the way, he passes a fast-food burger joint. The smell of grease wafts out. It smells artificial. It smells processed. It smells like corporate greed.

Skyler walks inside and orders a Number 1 with a Diet Coke.

He eats the burger. It is safe. It has been cooked to 165 degrees. The lettuce has been washed in a factory. The meat has been inspected by the USDA.

He is safe, wrapped in the warm embrace of the industrial system he claims to despise. He realizes, with a heavy heart, that he is not a Gatherer. He is a Consumer.

And as he wipes the ketchup from his lip, he checks his phone. The *PlantIdentify* app sends him a notification:

"Did you enjoy your find? Rate your Dandelion Greens!"

Skyler deletes the app.

This is the state of the modern human. We have traded the dangers of the wild for the safety of the sterile. We have lost the ability to feed ourselves, to identify food, or even to cook it. We are the first generation in history that would starve to death in a supermarket if the power went out, because we wouldn't know how to open the automatic doors manually.

We are soft. We are helpless. And we are full of Roundup.

But if you think our inability to feed ourselves is pathetic, just wait until you see how we handle conflict.

Because a full belly is only useful if you can keep it from getting kicked. And as we will see in the next chapter, the modern liberal has developed a defense mechanism that involves zero defense and 100% emotional manipulation.

Welcome to the Tribe of the Safe Space.

Chapter 4
The Tribe of "The Safe Space"

The Bubble Wrap Generation

To understand the precipitous decline of the human species, one must first understand the concept of **Antifragility**.

In nature, things that are stressed usually get stronger. If you expose a muscle to heavy weight, it tears and rebuilds itself denser. If you expose a bone to impact, it calcifies and hardens. If you expose a Grok to a harsh winter, he learns to sew a better coat or he freezes to death, thereby removing the "bad coat maker" gene from the pool.

Stress is the whetstone upon which humanity was sharpened.

The modern liberal, however, has declared war on stress. They believe that the human psyche is not a muscle to be exercised, but a vase made of spun sugar to be protected behind museum glass. They have embraced **Fragility** as a virtue.

To witness this phenomenon in its natural habitat, we must travel to the holiest of holy sites: The Modern University Campus.

Our protagonist, Skyler, has decided to audit a graduate-level seminar at Oberlin-Berkeley-Hampshire College. The course is titled: "Silence as Violence: Deconstructing the Patriarchal Implications of the Semicolon."

Skyler enters the lecture hall. It does not look like a place of rigorous intellectual debate. It looks like a daycare center for giant toddlers. The lighting is soft and non-threatening. The chairs are arranged in a circle to avoid the hierarchy of rows. There is a faint smell of lavender and anxiety.

The professor, a tenured academic named Dr. Willow (pronouns: Zhe/Zher), enters the room.

"Good morning, friends," Dr. Willow whispers. "Before we begin, let's do a temperature check. How are our spirits? Does anyone need to access the Cry Closet before we discuss the text?"

Skyler looks at the corner of the room. There is literally a closet padded with soundproofing foam, stocked with teddy bears and juice boxes. It is occupied. He can hear muffled sobbing.

"I'm feeling a bit raw," a student named Rain says. "I saw a truck with an American flag on it this morning. It felt very aggressive."

"I hold space for your pain," Dr. Willow nods gravely. "Let's take a collective deep breath to flush out that nationalism."

The class breathes.

In the Paleolithic era, a "threat" was a bear. In the modern era, a "threat" is a piece of cloth.

The lecture begins. Dr. Willow is explaining how the semicolon is a tool of oppression because it forces two independent clauses to coexist without their consent. Skyler is nodding furiously, taking notes on his iPad. This makes sense to him. Grammar is just another fence, and fences are bad.

But then, the unthinkable happens.

A student in the back row raises his hand. He is wearing a baseball cap (backward, which is strike one) and a t-shirt that says *Math is Real* (strike two). Let's call him Chad.

"Professor," Chad says, his voice dangerously normal volume. "Isn't a semicolon just a way to connect related ideas? I don't think it's oppressive. It's just punctuation."

The room goes silent. The silence is not peaceful; it is the silence of a bomb squad cutting the wrong wire.

Skyler stops typing. His heart hammers against his ribs. He has just witnessed **Dissent**.

In the wild, Dissent meant "I think we should hunt the mammoth from the left, not the right." If the dissenter was wrong, he got trampled. If he was right, the tribe ate. Dissent was a survival mechanism.

Here, Dissent is a biological weapon.

"Excuse me?" Dr. Willow asks, trembling. "Are you invalidating the lived experience of the sentence structure?"

"I'm just saying," Chad shrugs. "It's not that deep. It's grammar."

Pandemonium erupts.

Rain, the student who was traumatized by the flag, begins to hyperventilate. "He's gaslighting the text!" Rain screams. "He's centering logic over emotion! I feel unsafe!"

Skyler feels the panic rising in his own chest. He isn't afraid of Chad. Chad is 5'9" and holding a pencil. Skyler is afraid of the *ideas* Chad is presenting. The idea that reality might be objective. The idea that not everything is a power struggle. These thoughts are viruses, and Skyler has no immune system.

"Safe Space! Initiate Safe Space Protocol!" someone yells.

The class springs into action. Or rather, they spring into inaction.

Half the class drops to the floor and curls into the fetal position. This is the **Ostrich Maneuver**. If I cannot see the bad opinion, it cannot hurt me.

The other half begins to chant to drown out Chad's voice. "Words are violence! Silence is safety! Logic is a tool of the colonizer!"

Dr. Willow points a shaking finger at Chad. "You need to leave. You have triggered a trauma response in this community."

"I just like grammar," Chad says, confused.

"OUT!" the class screams in unison.

Chad gathers his bag and walks out, looking like a man who just accidentally walked into a cult meeting (which, effectively, he did).

As the door closes, the adrenaline dump hits Skyler. He is shaking. He feels like he just survived a war zone. He didn't, of course. He survived a mild disagreement. But to a creature that has been bred for fragility, a mild disagreement feels like a physical assault.

This is **Emotional Hemophilia**. The slightest scratch to the worldview causes uncontrollable bleeding.

Dr. Willow tries to regain control. "Okay, everyone. That was scary. That was a lot. Let's process. I'm going to pass around the Sensory Bin."

A plastic tub filled with uncooked rice and kinetic sand is passed around the circle. Skyler plunges his hands into the sand. He squeezes it. It is soft. It yields to him. It does not argue back.

This is better, he thinks. The sand understands me.

He looks around the room at his fellow future leaders of the free world. They are weeping, hugging stuffed animals, and playing with rice. They are twenty-five years old.

If a real crisis were to hit—say, a fire, a flood, or a foreign invasion—this room would not organize a defense. They would not form a bucket brigade. They would form a committee to discuss the tone of the fire alarm.

And they would burn.

But they would burn knowing that they never, ever let a semicolon oppress them.

The Trauma of the Tuesday Morning Meeting

Having survived the violence of the semicolon in college, Skyler eventually graduates. He enters the workforce.

In a functional society, the workforce is where the rubber meets the road. It is where results matter. If a bricklayer cries because the bricks are heavy, the wall does not get built. If a surgeon needs a mental health day in the middle of an appendectomy, the patient dies.

But Skyler does not go into bricklaying or surgery. Skyler gets a job as a "Junior Brand Narrative Architect" at a tech start-up called *Disruptr*.

Disruptr is not an office. It is an adult playpen designed to trick people into answering emails at 9:00 PM. There are ping-pong tables. There is a keg of cold-brew coffee. There are "nap pods" that look like giant plastic eggs.

Skyler feels safe here. The culture is curated. The vibes are immaculate.

Until the Tuesday Morning Stand-up Meeting.

The team gathers in a glass-walled conference room named "The Hive." The manager is a man named Rick. Rick is fifty years old. Rick remembers a time when you had to smoke cigarettes outside in the rain and type on computers that didn't have touch screens. Rick is the closest thing this office has to a Neanderthal.

Rick looks at Skyler.

"Skyler," Rick says, looking at a spreadsheet. "You didn't update the Q3 metrics yesterday. We needed those for the board meeting."

Skyler freezes.

In the wild, this is the equivalent of the Tribal Elder saying, *"You let the fire go out."* The appropriate response is: *"My bad. I will fix it."*

But Skyler has been trained to view **Accountability** as a form of **Aggression**.

"I... I didn't get to it," Skyler says, his voice wavering. "I was feeling a lot of bandwidth fatigue yesterday. The vibe was really heavy."

Rick blinks. "Bandwidth fatigue? Skyler, it's a spreadsheet. It takes ten minutes. I need you to do it now."

"Now?" Skyler asks. "Like... right now? In front of everyone?"

"Yes," Rick says. "We need the numbers."

Skyler's breathing becomes shallow. His Apple Watch taps his wrist: *High Heart Rate Detected.*

He is being put on the spot. He is being *perceived*. He is being asked to perform a task he failed to do.

"Rick," Skyler says, his voice dropping to a whisper. "Your tone is incredibly activating right now. You are centering productivity over my well-being. It feels very... toxic."

Rick sighs. It is the deep, rattling sigh of a man who just wants to retire and move to a cabin where there is no Wi-Fi.

"Skyler," Rick says. "I'm not trying to be toxic. I'm trying to run a business. Just update the sheet."

"I can't," Skyler says, standing up. "I'm having a trauma response to this demand. I need to remove myself from this environment."

Skyler runs out of the room. He flees to the Nap Pod. He curls up inside the plastic egg and closes the lid. He is safe. The spreadsheet cannot hurt him here.

In the Paleolithic era, if you ran away from your duty, the tribe starved. If you were the guy supposed to watch for wolves and you decided to take a nap because watching for wolves was "triggering," the wolves ate the baby. You would be cast out. You would die alone in the cold.

At *Disruptr*, Skyler is not cast out. He is coddled.

Ten minutes later, there is a gentle knock on the Nap Pod. It is not Rick. It is Ashley from HR.

Ashley is the High Priestess of the Safe Space. Her job is not to protect the company from lawsuits, but to protect the employees from reality.

"Skyler?" Ashley coos. "Can I come in? Or do you need more incubation time?"

"You can come in," Skyler sniffles.

Ashley opens the pod. She hands Skyler a LaCroix. "Rick told me what happened. I want you to know that we take psychological safety very seriously here. Rick has been cited for a micro-aggression."

"It felt like a *macro*-aggression," Skyler says, opening the LaCroix. "He used the imperative mood. He said 'Do it now.' It reminded me of my father."

"I am so sorry you had to relive that," Ashley says, taking notes on a tablet. "We are going to put you on a 'Restorative Work Path.' For the next week, you don't have to look at any spreadsheets. We want you to focus on self-care and maybe do some mood-boarding for the new logo."

"Thank you, Ashley," Skyler says. "I feel seen."

Meanwhile, back in the conference room, Rick is doing the spreadsheet himself.

This is the **parasitic nature of fragility**. The fragile members of the tribe do not contribute; they drain. They require constant maintenance. They consume the emotional and physical labor of the strong (Rick) while offering nothing but complaints about the tone in which the labor was requested.

But it gets worse.

The following day, Skyler decides that the office itself is the problem. The "open concept" layout is too exposing. The fluorescent lights are "hostile."

He files a request for "Remote Work Accommodation due to Sensory Processing Sensitivity."

He goes home. He creates his own personal Safe Space in his apartment. He buys blackout curtains. He buys a weighted blanket that weighs 25 pounds (essentially pinning him to the couch like a medieval torture device). He buys noise-canceling headphones.

He has constructed a womb.

He sits in the dark, under the heavy blanket, wearing headphones, staring at a screen.

He has achieved the ultimate goal of the modern liberal: **Total Insulation.**

He touches nothing real. He hears nothing real. He interacts with nothing real.

If a burglar were to break in, Skyler wouldn't hear him. If the fire alarm went off, Skyler wouldn't see the strobe light through his blackout curtains. If reality came knocking, Skyler would file a complaint with the universe's HR department.

He is "safe." But he is also effectively dead to the world. He has de-evolved from a creature that roamed the plains, battled the elements, and conquered the globe, into a soft, frightened lump of biomass hiding under a blanket, terrified of a 50-year-old man named Rick.

Grok, looking down from the great hunting grounds in the sky, is confused.

Why is he hiding? Grok asks. Is there a tiger?

No, the Universe replies. There was a spreadsheet.

Grok shakes his head. He turns away in shame.

But Skyler is not done. He has insulated his body, but he still needs to insulate his mind. The internet, after all, is full of people who disagree with him. And that simply cannot be allowed.

The Echo Chamber of Solitude

Skyler is now physically secure. He is in his apartment, under his weighted blanket, with his blackout curtains drawn. He has successfully eliminated the variables of weather, uncomfortable chairs, and managers named Rick.

But a threat remains. It is the glowing rectangle in his hand.

The internet is a dangerous place. It is filled with people who are wrong. Worse, it is filled with people who are *right* in a way that makes Skyler feel wrong.

He opens X (formerly Twitter). He scrolls.

His feed is mostly safe. It is a curated stream of people who look like him, vote like him, and have the same panic attacks as him. It is a digital warm bath.

But then, it happens. The algorithm, in a moment of glitchy malice, pushes a tweet into his timeline from outside his bubble.

It is a tweet from a user named @CommonSense45. The tweet reads: "I think it's okay for children to have competition. Losing builds character."

Skyler gasps.

The air in his apartment seems to thin. His heart flutters. He has been exposed to a **Harmful Idea**.

In a robust society, Skyler would read this, think *"I disagree,"* and keep scrolling. Or, if he were feeling feisty, he might reply with a counter-argument about the benefits of cooperative play.

But Skyler has no mental antibodies for this. He has lived in a sterile environment for so long that a single germ of disagreement threatens to kill him.

Losing builds character? Skyler thinks, horrified. That is literal violence. That is capitalist propaganda designed to justify the suffering of the non-winners.

He feels the urge to engage, but engagement is dangerous. If he replies, @CommonSense45 might reply back. And what if @CommonSense45 makes a good point? Skyler cannot risk that.

He reaches for the most powerful weapon in the modern liberal arsenal. It is not a club. It is not a spear.

It is the Block Button.

Tap.

@CommonSense45 vanishes.

Skyler lets out a breath he didn't know he was holding. "I am protecting my peace," he whispers. "I am curating my online experience."

But the fear lingers. If the algorithm showed him one Dissenter, there might be more. They are out there, lurking in the digital underbrush, waiting to jump out and suggest that maybe taxes are too high or that biology is real.

Skyler decides to go on the offensive. He downloads a browser extension called "BlockChain." It is a tool that allows him to preemptively block not just the person who tweeted the Bad Thing, but *everyone who follows them.*

It is the nuclear option. It is digital genocide.

He runs the script. Scanning... Blocking 14,000 users...

Skyler watches the numbers tick up. 5,000 blocked. 10,000 blocked. 14,000 human beings—people with families, jobs, and diverse opinions—are erased from Skyler's reality in seconds.

He feels a rush of power. He is God of this tiny universe. He decides who exists and who does not.

He refreshes his timeline.

It is beautiful. Tweet 1: *"Capitalism is the virus."* (100k likes) Tweet 2: *"Here is a picture of a frog that is gay."* (50k likes) Tweet 3: *"I am so tired."* (200k likes)

It is perfect. It is a seamless mirror reflecting his own neuroses back at him. There is no friction. There is no challenge. There is only **Affirmation**.

Skyler smiles. He types a status update: "Just did a massive block purge. If you can still see this, you are one of the good ones. The trash took itself out."

He waits for the likes. They roll in. *"So proud of you for setting boundaries,"* one reply says. *"Blocking is self-care,"* says another.

Skyler feels warm. He feels safe.

But let us zoom out and look at what Skyler has actually done.

Grok, the caveman, lived in a world of 360-degree danger. He had to look in all directions. He had to understand the wolf, the bear, and the rival tribe. Ignorance meant death.

Skyler has voluntarily blinded himself. He has built a cave with no entrance. He has painted the walls of the cave with pictures of people agreeing with him, and he sits in the center, rocking back and forth, telling himself that the tiger outside does not exist because he blocked it.

He has achieved **Intellectual Incest**. By only consuming ideas that are related to his own, his worldview has become inbred, deformed, and incapable of surviving in the wild.

He is "safe." But he is also stupid.

He has lost the ability to debate. He has lost the ability to persuade. He has lost the ability to understand *why* he believes what he believes, because he never has to defend it.

If you asked Skyler why he supports Policy X, he would say, "Because everyone I know supports it." If you asked him what the arguments against Policy X are, he would say, "I don't know, I blocked those people because they are fascists."

He is a leaf floating in a sewer, thinking he is navigating the ocean.

As the chapter closes, we leave Skyler in his dark apartment, under his heavy blanket, scrolling through a timeline that has been scrubbed of all humanity, save for the specific subset of humanity that is exactly as broken as he is.

He is the King of Nothing. The Mayor of Zero.

And he is happy. Until...

His stomach grumbles. The room gets a little cold. And a notification pops up on his screen.

It is a news alert. A new variant of a virus has been discovered. The government has issued new guidance.

Skyler perks up. His eyes widen.

He doesn't know how to hunt. He doesn't know how to fight. He doesn't know how to think. But he knows how to **Obey**.

The tribe needs a Shaman. And Skyler is ready to worship.

Chapter 5
The Shaman and The Science

The High Priest of the Screen

Anthropologists tell us that every primitive tribe had a Shaman.

The Shaman was a figure of immense power. He was usually the guy who was too physically weak to hunt the mammoth and too chemically unstable to gather the berries without eating the hallucinogenic ones. So, he found a niche: He claimed to speak for the Gods.

If the rain didn't fall, the Shaman would shake a bag of dried bones, dance around a fire, and declare that the Sun God was angry because Oog didn't share his antelope meat. The tribe, terrified of starving, would give the Shaman the best cut of meat, and lo and behold, eventually it would rain.

The Shaman didn't understand meteorology. He understood **leverage**.

Fast forward 20,000 years. We like to think we have outgrown such superstition. We have microscopes. We have peer review. We have data.

But look closely at Skyler.

Skyler is sitting cross-legged on his floor (his couch is covered in laundry he is too depressed to fold). He is staring at his 55-inch OLED television with the same rapture Grok reserved for a solar eclipse.

On the screen is a man in a white lab coat. Let's call him Dr. Glimmer.

Dr. Glimmer is the Director of the Department of Public Wellness and Safety. He is 84 years old. He has not treated a patient since the Nixon administration. He has, however, survived fourteen different presidencies by mastering the art of saying absolutely nothing in five hundred words or more.

Dr. Glimmer is the modern Shaman. And Skyler is his most devout acolyte.

"The data is evolving," Dr. Glimmer says, his voice raspy and authoritative. "We now recommend that in addition to social distancing, you should hold your breath whenever you pass a mailbox. The mail is a vector for... bad vibes."

Skyler nods frantically. "Hold breath at mailbox," he mutters, typing it into his Notes app. "Makes sense. The aerosol transmission via postage stamps is undeniable."

Does it make sense? No. Is there any study proving that mailboxes emit viral particles? No.

But Skyler does not practice *science* (lowercase s). Science is a method of inquiry involving hypothesis, testing, and skepticism.

Skyler practices **The Science**™ (capital S).

The Science™ is not a method; it is a theology. It is a belief system where Truth is revealed not by evidence, but by Authority. If Dr. Glimmer says gravity is suspended on Tuesdays, Skyler will float around his apartment on Tuesday, or at least pretend to, so he doesn't look like a "Gravity Denier."

In the Paleolithic era, Grok was a skeptic by necessity. If the Shaman said, "This red berry is safe," Grok would watch the Shaman eat it first. If the Shaman didn't die, Grok would eat it. If the Shaman started foaming at the mouth, Grok would find a new Shaman.

Skyler, however, has lost this survival instinct. He operates on **Blind Faith**.

Dr. Glimmer continues. "We are also suggesting that you wear two masks. No, three. Actually, just wrap your head in Saran Wrap. But poke a hole for a straw so you can stay hydrated."

"Three masks," Skyler whispers. "Of course. It's simple math. Three is better than one."

He runs to his bathroom. He finds his stash of N95s. He puts one on. He puts a cloth mask with a pattern of Ruth Bader Ginsburg's face over it. He puts a surgical mask over that.

He looks in the mirror. He looks like a hostage in a bank robbery movie. He can barely breathe. His glasses fog up instantly.

"I am protecting the community," he wheezes.

He is not protecting the community. He is suffocating himself to signal his virtue.

This is the key difference between the Primitive and the Progressive. The Primitive did things to *survive*. The Progressive does things to *belong*.

Skyler's phone buzzes. It is a notification from a news site: *New Study Suggests Sunlight May Help Immunity.*

Skyler frowns. This information is confusing. Sunlight is free. Sunlight is natural. Dr. Glimmer didn't mention sunlight. Dr. Glimmer mentioned staying inside and waiting for the government to mail him a solution.

Skyler checks Twitter to see what the consensus is.

The hashtag #SunlightIsRightWing is trending.

"Oh," Skyler says. "I see. Promoting sunlight is ableist against people who live in basements. It's also adjacent to tanning bed culture, which is problematic."

He closes the blinds. He rejects the literal source of all life on Earth because the algorithm told him it was politically suspect.

This is the Death of Observation.

Grok knew the sun was good because it made him warm. He knew the rain was wet because he felt it. His reality was empirical.

Skyler's reality is curated. If his eyes tell him one thing ("The sun feels nice"), but the Shaman tells him another ("The sun is a vector for misinformation"), he will gouge out his own eyes to remain faithful to the tribe.

He returns to the TV. Dr. Glimmer is now holding up a chart. The chart has a red line going up. It looks scary.

"We must flatten the curve," Dr. Glimmer intones. "By flattening your spirit."

"Flatten the spirit," Skyler repeats. "Yes. Joy is a luxury we cannot afford right now."

He looks at his guitar in the corner. He hasn't played it in months. Playing music spreads droplets. Playing music implies happiness. Happiness is inappropriate during a Crisis.

He puts the guitar in the closet.

He sits back down. He waits for the next commandment.

He is a vessel. He is empty of critical thought, filled only with the latest guidance. He is the perfect citizen of the decline: docile, frightened, and waiting for permission to live.

But the ritual isn't just about listening. It's about *doing*. And in Part 2, we will see Skyler venture out into the world, armed with his Talismans of Safety, ready to judge the heretics.

The Inquisition of the One-Way Aisle

Armed with the spiritual armor of Dr. Glimmer's latest decree, Skyler prepares to leave his apartment. He is not going to hunt, nor to gather. He is going on a **Patrol**.

He clips a bottle of hand sanitizer to his belt loop. In the days of yore, a warrior carried a sword to ward off enemies. Skyler carries a 2-ounce bottle of alcohol gel to ward off reality. It is his Holy Water. He does not use it to clean his hands; he uses it to anoint himself in a Rite of Purification.

Squirt. Rub. Sting.

He feels cleaner. He feels righteous.

He heads to the local pharmacy. He is not sick, but he needs to buy more rapid tests. Skyler tests himself every morning, not because he has symptoms, but because the test is a daily confessional. A single red line means he is pure. Two red lines mean he has sinned and must be cast into the leper colony (his bedroom).

He enters the store. Immediately, he looks down.

The floor is covered in stickers. Red arrows. Blue circles. Instructions on where to stand. *Stand Here. Do Not Stand Here. Walk This Way.*

To a confused alien—or a caveman—this would look like a ritual dance floor. To Skyler, this is **Sacred Geometry**.

He approaches Aisle 4 (Toothpaste and Deodorant). He needs sensitive-teeth whitening strips. But there is a problem.

The arrow on the floor points *away* from him.

Aisle 4 is a "Down" aisle. Skyler is currently at the "Up" end.

The toothpaste is ten feet away. There is no one else in the aisle. The air is still. The risk of viral transmission is zero.

Grok would walk ten feet, grab the toothpaste, and leave. Grok understands physics: The shortest distance between two points is a straight line.

Skyler, however, is paralyzed. To walk against the arrow is to challenge The Science™. To walk against the arrow is to admit that the arrow is just a sticker placed by a tired teenager earning minimum wage, rather than a magical barrier erected by epidemiologists.

He sighs. He turns around. He walks down Aisle 5 (Shampoo), turns left, walks past the pharmacy counter, turns left again, and enters Aisle 4 from the "correct" side.

He has walked 200 feet to move 10 feet. He has wasted calories and time. But he feels a warm glow in his chest. He followed the rules. He is a Good Boy.

But his pilgrimage is interrupted.

As he reaches for the whitening strips, he sees *Him*.

A man. Let's call him Steve.

Steve is wearing a flannel shirt. He is not wearing a mask. And—horror of horrors—Steve is walking *up* the *down* aisle.

Skyler gasps into his three masks. The sound is a muffled *mphhhff.*

Steve is violating the Sacred Geometry. He is walking directly toward Skyler, breathing the air, existing in a state of chaotic rebellion.

In a tribal society, if someone violated a taboo (like peeing on the sacred fire), the tribe would confront him. They would shout. They might throw rocks.

Skyler does not throw rocks. Skyler throws shade.

He stiffens his posture. He widens his eyes to convey judgment (the only part of his face Steve can see). He presses his back against the shelving unit, knocking over a display of travel-sized mouthwash, to create the maximum amount of social distance.

"Excuse me," Skyler says, his voice muffled by the layers of fabric.

Steve stops. He looks at Skyler. "Yeah?"

"You're going the wrong way," Skyler says, pointing a trembling finger at the floor sticker. "The arrow. It points that way."

Steve looks at the floor. He looks at the toothpaste in his hand. He looks at Skyler.

"I just needed toothpaste, buddy," Steve says.

"It doesn't matter what you *need*," Skyler snaps. "It matters what the guidelines say. You are compromising the traffic flow. You are creating a vector event."

Steve blinks. "A vector event? I'm grabbing Crest."

"You are breathing on me!" Skyler shrieks (quietly, so as not to expel droplets).

"I'm six feet away," Steve says.

"Six feet is the minimum!" Skyler recites. "Dr. Glimmer said we should act as if *everyone* is infected. You are infected. I am infected. The toothpaste is infected!"

Steve looks at Skyler with a mixture of amusement and pity. This is the look a wolf gives a domesticated poodle that is barking from behind a glass door.

"You need to relax," Steve says. "Take a breath. Maybe take off one of those masks. You look like you're about to pass out."

"I will not relax!" Skyler says. "Relaxing is how the virus wins! Vigilance is survival!"

Steve shakes his head. "Alright, man. Good luck with... whatever this is."

Steve walks past him. He brushes within *four feet* of Skyler.

Skyler holds his breath. He squeezes his eyes shut. He imagines the viral particles swarming around him like angry bees. He waits for death.

He counts to thirty. He exhales. He is still alive.

But he is shaken. He has witnessed a Heretic. A man who looked at the Shaman's stickers and said, "No." And the earth did not open up to swallow him. Lightning did not strike him.

This is a dangerous realization for Skyler. If the stickers don't work... what else doesn't work?

He pushes the thought away. No, he tells himself. Steve got lucky. Steve is a ticking time bomb. I am safe because I obeyed the arrow.

He grabs his whitening strips. He rushes to the checkout.

He needs to report this. Not to the police—they are problematic—but to the Manager. The Manager is the local chieftain of the store. The Manager controls the loudspeaker.

He finds a teenage employee named Kyle who is staring at his phone.

"Excuse me," Skyler says urgently. "There was a man in Aisle 4. He was going the wrong way. He was unmasked. He was... breathing aggressively."

Kyle looks up. "Okay?"

"You need to do something," Skyler says. "You need to enforce the protocols."

"Dude," Kyle says. "I make twelve dollars an hour. I'm not fighting a guy in a flannel shirt."

Skyler is aghast. The system is failing. The Shaman's decrees are being ignored by the foot soldiers.

He buys his items. He runs to his car. He locks the doors.

He grabs his sanitizer. *Squirt. Rub. Sting.*

He pulls out his phone. He opens the neighborhood "NextDoor" app. This is the digital town square where the tribe gathers to point fingers.

He types furiously: **ALERT: BIOTERRORIST AT CVS.** "I just witnessed a man blatantly disregarding the directional signage in Aisle 4. No mask. Hostile attitude. I felt fearing for my life. Avoid the toothpaste aisle for at least 72 hours until the aerosols settle. We are in this together, even if some people want us to die."

He hits post.

Within seconds, the likes roll in. "Thank you for your vigilance, Skyler!" "I'm shaking just reading this." "We need a lockdown!"

Skyler leans back in his seat. He feels better. He didn't stop Steve. He didn't fix the problem. But he *signaled* his loyalty to the tribe.

He starts his electric car. He drives home alone, wearing his three masks, terrified of the air, terrified of his neighbors, but secure in the knowledge that he is on the Right Side of History.

Meanwhile, Steve is at home brushing his teeth, completely unaware that he is a bioterrorist.

This is the legacy of the Shaman. He hasn't cured the disease. He has created a new one: A mental illness where obedience is valued over results, and common sense is treated as heresy.

But if you think Skyler's relationship with "The Science" is bad, wait until you see his relationship with self-defense.

In the next chapter, we explore what happens when the tribe decides that the only thing more dangerous than a criminal is the weapon you might use to stop him.

Chapter 6
Disarming the Tribe

The Sharp Rock Theory

In the beginning, there was the Rock.

It was a heavy, blunt instrument. Grok, our ancestor, picked it up and realized a fundamental truth of the universe: *If I hold this, and the wolf does not, I win.*

Then, Grok got smarter. He chipped the edges of the rock. He made it sharp. He tied it to a stick. Suddenly, Grok wasn't just fighting off wolves; he was keeping the neighboring tribe from stealing his fire and his women. The weapon was the Great Equalizer. It allowed the weak to defend themselves against the strong. It turned a prey species into an Apex Predator.

For 200,000 years, the rule of survival was simple: **Stay Armed.**

Enter Skyler.

Skyler lives in a world that is safer than Grok's by every statistical metric, yet Skyler is more terrified of weapons than Grok was of a thunderstorm. Skyler believes in a new, radical theory of physics: **Inanimate Object Agency.**

Skyler believes that weapons have souls. Evil, possessed souls. He believes that if you put a gun on a table, it might spontaneously stand up, grow legs, and rob a liquor store. He believes that the mere presence of a tool causes violence, rather than the intent of the user.

To Skyler, the Sharp Rock is the enemy. If we just ban all the sharp rocks, the wolves will agree to a ceasefire.

It is 2:00 AM on a Tuesday. Skyler is asleep in his womb-like apartment. Suddenly, there is a sound.

CRASH.

The sound of breaking glass. It is coming from the living room.

In the Paleolithic era, this sound (a twig snapping) would trigger an immediate, violent response. Grok would grab his club. His adrenaline would dump. He would be ready to smash a skull to protect his cave.

Skyler wakes up. His heart hammers. But his brain does not reach for a weapon. His brain reaches for a **Nuance**.

Is that a burglar? Skyler thinks. No, we don't use that word. That is a 'Justice-Impacted Individual seeking unauthorized entry.'

Skyler sits up. He needs to defend himself. He scans the room for a tool.

He does not own a gun. Guns are for people who drive pickup trucks and don't listen to NPR. Guns are "icky." He does not own a baseball bat. He played soccer as a kid (where they didn't keep score), and he doesn't own any sports equipment that could be weaponized. He has a heavy hydro-flask water bottle. It is covered in stickers that say *Be Kind* and *Coexist*.

He grabs the water bottle.

He creeps to the bedroom door. He can hear footsteps in the living room. Heavy, booted footsteps.

Skyler's internal monologue begins to race. It is not a tactical monologue; it is a sociological one.

Why is he here? Skyler asks himself. Is it because of poverty? Is it because of the school-to-prison pipeline? If I confront him with violence, am I just perpetuating the cycle of trauma?

Skyler decides that he will not escalate. He will de-escalate. He will use his words. He has taken a seminar on "Non-Violent Communication." He is ready.

He opens the door.

Standing in his living room is a man wearing a ski mask (not for COVID reasons) and holding a crowbar. The man is unplugging Skyler's PS5.

"Excuse me!" Skyler squeaks.

The burglar freezes. He looks at Skyler. He sees a man in flannel pajama bottoms holding a water bottle like a holy relic. The burglar is not intimidated.

"Hey," the burglar says. "Go back to bed."

This is a direct command. It establishes dominance. Grok would have thrown the spear at this moment.

Skyler, however, tries to establish a dialogue.

"I... I want to acknowledge your pain," Skyler says, his voice shaking. "I understand that systemic inequality has led you to this moment. You aren't bad. The system is bad."

The burglar blinks behind the mask. "What?"

"I don't care about the PlayStation," Skyler lies (he cares deeply about the PlayStation). "It's just material goods. But I want you to know that stealing this won't fill the void inside you. Only restorative justice can do that."

The burglar disconnects the HDMI cable. "Okay, buddy. Thanks for the therapy."

"Wait!" Skyler steps forward. "Do you need food? I have some organic quinoa in the pantry. I can make you a bowl. We can talk about the root causes of your desperation."

The burglar laughs. It is a harsh, mocking laugh. He walks toward Skyler, raising the crowbar.

"Sit down," the burglar says.

Skyler sits. He sits immediately. His instinct to submit is stronger than his instinct to survive. He has been trained that "fighting back" is what toxic males do. Fighting back leads to injury. Fighting back is *rude*.

The burglar walks past him, grabs Skyler's laptop off the desk, and heads for the window.

"Please," Skyler whispers. "I have a screenplay on there."

"Back it up to the cloud next time," the burglar advises, and climbs out the window.

Skyler is left alone. He is unharmed physically. But he has been stripped of his property and his dignity.

Now, he faces the ultimate Liberal Dilemma: **The Police Call.**

Skyler hates the police. He has a sign in his window that says *DEFUND*. He has tweeted at least fifty times that police are state-sponsored oppressors.

But now, his PS5 is gone.

He looks at his phone. He looks at the number 9-1-1.

If he calls, he is a hypocrite. He is inviting the "armed agents of the state" into his home to hunt down a marginalized person. If he doesn't call, he has no police report, and his renter's insurance won't pay out.

It is a battle between Ideology and Economics.

Economics wins. It always does.

Skyler dials 911.

"911, what is your emergency?"

"Hi," Skyler whispers. "I... I had a break-in."

"Are you safe?"

"Yes. He left. He took my gaming console and my laptop."

"We'll send an officer over to take a report."

"Wait," Skyler says. "Um... can you send a... nice officer? Like, one who has done sensitivity training? And maybe... tell him not to bring his gun? Or at least keep it in the car?"

"Sir," the dispatcher says, "the officers are armed."

"Okay, but... the suspect is a victim of society," Skyler pleads. "I don't want him *hurt*. I just want my laptop back. Can we send a social worker to find him?"

"We don't have tactical social workers, sir. An officer is on the way."

Skyler hangs up. He feels dirty. He feels like a traitor to the cause. He has invoked the power of the State to protect his private property.

He goes to the window. He looks out at the city.

Somewhere out there, the burglar is laughing. The burglar has a crowbar. The burglar has a PS5. The burglar has won.

The burglar is operating on the Old Rules: *Might makes right.* Skyler is operating on the New Rules: *Weakness makes virtue.*

The problem, as Skyler is beginning to suspect, is that the Old Rules still apply to everyone who isn't in Skyler's book club. The world is still full of wolves. And Skyler has voluntarily pulled out his own teeth.

But the disarmament isn't just physical. It's psychological. The modern liberal hasn't just thrown away the gun; they have thrown away the very concept of "The Enemy." They believe that everyone is just a friend they haven't apologized to yet.

In Part 2, we will see what happens when Skyler decides to take a self-defense class designed for people who are afraid of their own shadows.

The Way of the Passive Warrior

Shaken by the loss of his PlayStation and the shattering of his illusion of safety, Skyler decides he must learn to defend himself.

However, he cannot join a traditional martial arts gym. He looked into a local Boxing gym, but it smelled of sweat and unaddressed rage. The instructor yelled. There was sparring. People were hitting each other *on purpose*. Skyler found the environment "hyper-masculine" and "exclusionary to bodies of softness."

He looked into Brazilian Jiu-Jitsu, but the idea of a "stranglehold" felt problematic. Strangling implies silencing, and Skyler believes in amplifying voices, not cutting off their air supply.

So, he finds a dojo that aligns with his values.

It is held in the back of a vegan bakery on Tuesday nights. The class is called: **"Empowered Boundaries: Kinetic De-escalation for Empaths."**

Skyler enters the room. Everyone is barefoot. The instructor is a man named Sage. Sage is thin, wispy, and wearing pants made of hemp that seem to be held up by hope alone. Sage does not look like he could fight off a cold, let alone an attacker, but his bio says he is a "Black Belt in Conflict Transformation."

"Welcome, warriors of peace," Sage whispers. "Tonight, we are not learning to fight. Fighting is a failure of the imagination. We are learning to create a 'No' so powerful that the universe obeys it."

Skyler nods. This resonates. He wants a magical 'No.' He doesn't want to learn how to throw a punch, because punching hurts his knuckles.

"First," Sage says, "we must ask for consent. Turn to your partner. Look them in the eye. Ask, 'May I enter your kinetic sphere to practice boundary setting?'"

Skyler turns to his partner, a woman named Fern who is wearing a t-shirt that says *Plants Have Feelings Too*.

"May I enter your kinetic sphere?" Skyler asks.

"You may," Fern says solemnly. "But please be mindful of my shoulder. I carry a lot of ancestral trauma there."

"Understood," Skyler says.

They begin the drills.

In a functional combat class, you learn to target vulnerable areas: the nose, the throat, the groin. You learn to inflict maximum damage in minimum time. In Sage's class, they learn **"The Wall of Consent."**

"Hold your hand up," Sage instructs. "Palm out. This is the universal symbol for 'Stop.' Channel your energy into your palm. Visualize a forcefield of pure autonomy."

Skyler holds his hand up. He imagines a forcefield. He feels powerful.

"Now," Sage says. "Your partner will walk toward you slowly, manifesting 'Aggressive Energy.' You will stop them with your voice and your palm."

Fern walks toward Skyler. She is walking at the speed of a sloth on sedatives. She does not look aggressive; she looks like she is browsing a museum.

"Stop!" Skyler says firmly (but not too loud). "I do not consent to this interaction!"

Fern stops. She smiles. "Wow," she says. "I really felt that. You held space for your own safety."

Skyler beams. It worked. Fern stopped.

Of course, Fern stopped because she is a nice person participating in a role-playing exercise. The burglar with the crowbar was not Fern. If Skyler had held up his palm to the burglar and shouted about consent, the burglar likely would have high-fived his face with the crowbar.

But Skyler doesn't know this. Skyler thinks he has unlocked a superpower.

Next, they practice **"The Escape."**

"If the aggressor grabs you," Sage says, "do not struggle. Struggling feeds their aggression. Instead, go limp. Become like water. Make yourself 'heavy' with the weight of your moral superiority."

Sage demonstrates. A student grabs Sage's wrist. Sage slumps to the floor like a wet towel. The student, confused, lets go.

"See?" Sage says from the floor. "He could not hold me. I removed myself from the equation."

Skyler takes notes mentally. *Go limp. Be a wet towel.*

In the wild, going limp is what a possum does. It is a gamble that the predator will lose interest. Sometimes it works. Usually, the coyote just eats the possum while it's lying there.

Skyler practices going limp. Fern grabs his arm. Skyler collapses. Fern giggles. "You're so heavy!"

"It's the weight of my convictions," Skyler says from the floorboards.

The final drill is the most important: **The Verbal stun.**

"Words are weapons," Sage says. "If an attacker comes at you, you must disrupt their narrative. You must say something that breaks their script of violence."

"Like what?" a student asks. "Like 'Fire'?"

"No," Sage says. "Fire creates panic. You should shout something that invites introspection. Something like, 'WHO HURT YOU?' or 'I SEE YOUR PAIN!'"

Skyler practices this. He imagines a mugger running at him with a knife.

Skyler strikes a pose. He thrusts his palm out. He shouts: "I VALIDATE YOUR TRAUMA!"

The class applauds.

"Beautiful," Sage says. "You turned the aggression back on itself. You offered them therapy in the moment of conflict. That is true mastery."

The class ends with a group hum to "re-center the energy." Skyler pays his $40 drop-in fee. He walks out into the night feeling invincible.

He walks down the street. It is dark. He sees a shadow move in an alleyway.

His heart jumps. But this time, he is prepared. He has the tools. He has the Wall of Consent. He has the Wet Towel Defense. He has the Verbal Stun.

He walks past the alley. A stray cat jumps out, hissing.

Skyler instinctively throws up his hand. "STOP!" he yells. "I DO NOT CONSENT!"

The cat stares at him. It hisses again and runs away.

Skyler exhales. "It works," he whispers. "I am a warrior."

He has successfully deterred a six-pound feline. He equates this with combat readiness.

He goes home to his apartment (which now lacks a PlayStation). He sleeps soundly, believing that he is prepared for the wolves.

But the wolves are not cats. And the wolves do not care about his kinetic sphere.

Skyler has completed his disarmament. He has replaced the gun with the phone (to call the police). He has replaced the police with the social worker. And now, he has replaced the fight-or-flight response with a lecture on trauma.

He is a walking, talking appetizer for the real world.

But surely, Skyler thinks, the Government will protect me. Even if I can't fight, the State is the ultimate Alpha, right?

In the next chapter, we will see what happens when Skyler puts his full faith in the "Nanny State" to solve a problem that requires actual, rugged individualism.

We are going to visit the DMV of the Apocalypse.

Chapter 7
The Nanny State Cave

The Comfort of Red Tape

Freedom is a terrifying concept.

For Grok, freedom was absolute. He could walk anywhere. He could sleep anywhere. He could eat anything he could kill. But this freedom came with a heavy price: Total Responsibility. If Grok made a mistake—if he walked off a cliff or ate a poisonous frog—there was no one to sue. There was no Ombudsman to file a complaint with. There was just gravity and death.

To the modern liberal, this level of responsibility is paralyzing. They look at the vast, open horizon of human potential and think, *Can we put a guardrail up? And maybe a warning sign? And a permit fee?*

Skyler is currently facing a crisis of responsibility.

The window in his living room is still broken from the burglar's exit in the previous chapter. A cold draft is blowing in. A normal human response—the "Rugged Individual" response—would be to go to the hardware store, buy a piece of plexiglass, and duct tape it up until a glazier can arrive.

But Skyler knows better. Skyler lives in a **Sanctuary City of Bureaucracy**.

He knows that to touch the exterior of his building is to invite the wrath of the Gods (The Zoning Board).

He logs onto the city's web portal. It is a website designed in 2004, powered by a server that runs on a hamster wheel. It crashes twice. Finally, he finds the form: **Application for Fenestration Modification in a Historic-Adjacent Zone (Form 27B-6).**

Most people would look at this form and groan. Skyler looks at it and sighs with relief.

Here, in the rows of empty boxes and drop-down menus, Skyler feels held. The form tells him exactly what to do. It asks for his name, his address, his tax ID, his carbon footprint estimation, and a sworn affidavit that the glass he intends to use is "Bird-Safe" and "Ethically Sourced."

He fills it out with the diligence of a monk transcribing scripture.

- **Question 14:** *Will the repair involve the use of fossil-fuel powered tools?*
- **Skyler's Answer:** *No. I will use a hand-cranked screwdriver and positive affirmations.*

He hits submit. A message pops up: "Your application has been received. Estimated processing time: 6-8 weeks. Do not attempt repair until approved. Violation penalty: $5,000."

Skyler sits back. 6-8 weeks.

He looks at the hole in his window. It is currently 45 degrees outside.

A libertarian would scream. A conservative would just fix the window and not tell anyone.

Skyler, however, feels a strange sense of virtue. By freezing in his apartment for two months, he is **Respecting the Process**. He is acknowledging that the State knows best. The State is the Parent, and he is the Child. The Parent says, "Wait," so the Child waits.

He tapes a garbage bag over the window. It flaps loudly in the wind.

Two weeks pass. The garbage bag tears. Skyler replaces it.

Then, a letter arrives. It is on thick, official stationery. It is from the **Department of Neighborhood Aesthetics and Compliance**.

Skyler opens it with trembling hands. Has he been approved? Can he finally stop wearing three sweaters indoors?

He reads the letter:

"Dear Resident/Occupant, We have noticed an unauthorized polyethylene membrane (garbage bag) adhered to your domicile. This material is not on the approved list of Historic Facade Coverings. Furthermore, the flapping sound exceeds the auditory nuisance threshold of 50 decibels. You are hereby summoned to a hearing at the Department of Compliance. Please bring proof of residency, a photo ID, and a check for the $250 citation."

Skyler gasps. He is in trouble.

But strangely, he isn't angry. He doesn't think, *This is tyranny.* He thinks, *I have been naughty.*

He feels a rush of submissive adrenaline. The State is paying attention to him! The State cares enough about his window to fine him. It is a twisted form of love.

He prepares for his court date like it's a job interview. He shaves. He puts on a "responsible" cardigan. He prints out his documents in triplicate.

He travels to the Department of Compliance. It is a brutalist concrete building that looks like a Soviet bunker designed by a depressed architect.

He enters. The line is long. It moves slowly. The air is stale.

To Skyler, this is the Cathedral. The fluorescent lights are the stained glass. The "Take a Number" machine is the altar.

He takes a number: **G-452**. The screen currently reads: **A-004**.

He sits down on a hard plastic chair bolted to the floor. He waits.

An hour passes. Two hours.

Next to him sits a man in dirty work boots. Let's call him Ron. Ron looks like he builds things with his hands. Ron looks miserable.

"Can you believe this?" Ron grumbles. "I just want to build a deck on my own property. I've been here three times. It's a joke."

Skyler straightens his cardigan. He feels the need to defend the Nanny.

"It's not a joke," Skyler whispers reverently. "It's the price of civilization. Without these rules, people would just build decks anywhere. It would be anarchy. Imagine... decks touching other decks. The chaos."

Ron looks at Skyler. "It's my backyard, kid."

"It's *our* backyard," Skyler corrects him. "We are a collective. The government is just the things we choose to do together."

"I didn't choose to wait four hours to pay a guy to tell me my wood is the wrong color," Ron spits.

Skyler turns away. Ron doesn't get it. Ron thinks he is an individual. Skyler knows the truth: **We are all just inventory in the State's warehouse.** And inventory needs to be counted, stamped, and managed.

Finally, Skyler's number is called.

He approaches the glass partition. Behind it sits a bureaucrat named Brenda. Brenda has not smiled since 1998. She wields a rubber stamp like a weapon of war.

"Name?" Brenda asks, without looking up.

"Skyler," he says. "I'm here about the garbage bag incident."

"Citation number?"

He hands it over.

Brenda types for a solid minute. She stops. She sighs. She types again.

"You didn't file the T-14 Temporary Shading Permit," Brenda says. "That's why you got fined."

"I didn't know," Skyler apologizes. "I'm so sorry. I want to comply. Tell me how to comply."

"You need to pay the fine," Brenda says. "Then you need to file the T-14. Then you need to wait for the Fenestration Approval. Then you can fix the window."

"Okay," Skyler says. "I can pay. Do you take Apple Pay?"

"Check or money order only," Brenda says. "And fill out this form acknowledging your guilt."

She slides a piece of paper under the glass. It is a confession.

I, the undersigned, admit that I attempted to mitigate a draft without state supervision. I acknowledge that my comfort is secondary to the aesthetic cohesion of the neighborhood.

Skyler signs it. He writes a check.

"Thank you, Brenda," Skyler says. "Thank you for keeping us safe from unauthorized garbage bags."

Brenda looks at him. For a second, her eyes flicker with confusion. She is used to people yelling. She is used to people crying. She is not used to people *thanking* her for the boot on their neck.

"Next," she barks.

Skyler walks out of the building. He is $250 poorer. His window is still broken. He still has to wait 6 weeks.

But he feels **Safe**.

The System works. He was punished for his transgression, and now he is back on the path of righteousness. He has outsourced his judgment to Brenda. He doesn't have to decide what is right or wrong; the code tells him.

He gets on the bus. He sees an ad for a politician promising "Universal Pre-K, Universal Healthcare, and Universal Housing."

Skyler swoons. Universal Everything, he thinks. A world where I never have to make a choice again. A world where the Nanny tucks me in, feeds me, and tells me when to wake up.

He closes his eyes and dreams of the ultimate Nanny State Cave: A padded room where the government chews his food for him, just to make sure he doesn't choke.

The Internet of Things That Hate You

Skyler returns to his "Smart Apartment."

In the Neolithic era, a man's home was his castle (or at least his very defensible pile of rocks). Inside the cave, the rules of the outside world did not apply. If Grok wanted to paint a bison on the wall, he painted a bison. If he wanted to eat an entire leg of venison at 3:00 AM, no one stopped him. The cave was the one place where the individual was Sovereign.

Skyler's apartment, however, is not a castle. It is a **Panopticon of Benevolence.**

Every device in his home is connected to the internet. Every device has a name. Every device has a "Safety Protocol" designed to protect Skyler from his own poor decision-making.

Skyler is hungry. The stress of the Department of Compliance has burned calories. He wants comfort food. He wants the forbidden fruit: A pint of non-dairy, but high-sugar, "Chunky Monkey" ice cream substitute.

He approaches his refrigerator. The fridge is a $4,000 monolith named **Gaia.** It has a touch screen, a camera inside that identifies food, and a direct uplink to his health insurance provider.

Skyler grabs the handle. It is locked.

A soft, maternal voice emanates from the speaker.

"I'm sorry, Skyler. I can't let you do that."

Skyler sighs. "Gaia, open the door. I want the ice cream."

"I've detected a spike in your cortisol levels," Gaia responds soothingly. "Stress-eating is a maladaptive coping mechanism. Also, your Bio-Ring indicates you have not met your movement goals for the day. You are currently in a Caloric Surplus Zone."

"I don't care," Skyler whines. "It's my food. I bought it."

"Technically," Gaia corrects him, "you subscribed to the food. And under the terms of your 'Wellness Plus' municipal health plan, access to high-sugar items is restricted between the hours of 8:00 AM and 6:00 PM. Would you like a celery stick? I can unlock the crisper drawer."

Skyler slumps against the stainless steel. He is a grown man. He has a beard (sort of). And he is being bullied by a kitchen appliance.

In a free society, Skyler would unplug the fridge. He would take a crowbar (if the burglar hadn't stolen it) and pry the door open. He would reclaim his liberty.

But Skyler has been conditioned to believe that **Restriction is Care**.

Gaia is right, he thinks. I don't need the sugar. The sugar is poison. The fridge loves me. The fridge wants me to live forever.

"Okay, Gaia," he whispers submissively. "Unlock the celery."

Click. The crisper drawer pops open. The rest of the fridge remains sealed.

Skyler eats his sad, lukewarm celery. He feels "supported."

He walks into the living room. It is getting dark. The garbage bag over the window is flapping. He decides to turn on the lamp.

Flick.

Nothing happens. The bulb has burned out.

In the 20th century, this was a minor inconvenience. You went to the closet, grabbed a $0.50 incandescent bulb, screwed it in, and let there be light.

But Skyler lives in the Green Utopia. Incandescent bulbs are illegal. They are "energy vampires." Even standard LEDs are frowned upon.

Skyler needs a **Smart Bulb**.

He goes to his supply closet. He finds a box for a "Lumen-X 5000: The Bulb with a Brain." He takes out the bulb. It looks like a small spaceship.

He screws it in. He waits for the light.

Instead, the bulb begins to pulse red.

He pulls out his phone. He opens the *Lumen-X* app. **Status:** *Firmware Update Required.* **Estimated Download Time:** *45 minutes.*

Skyler sits on the floor in the dark, watching a progress bar on his phone. He cannot have light until the lightbulb updates its software.

Why does a lightbulb need software? a sane person might ask. To track your usage, the Nanny State answers. To dim automatically during 'Peak Grid Strain.' To change color to 'Calming Blue' if the Prime Minister declares a National Mood Emergency.

Skyler waits. The download fails at 98%.

Error: WiFi signal weak. Please move the router closer to the lamp.

Skyler groans. He moves the router. He restarts the download.

While he waits, he gets cold. The wind from the broken window is biting. He approaches his thermostat, the **Nest-Mother**.

"Nest-Mother," Skyler says. "Set temperature to 72 degrees."

The thermostat's screen glows orange. *"Request Denied,"* it says.

"Why?" Skyler chatters.

"The Regional Energy Equity Board has declared a 'Solidarity Hour,'" the thermostat explains. "To show support for those less fortunate who do not have heating, all connected thermostats have been capped at 64 degrees for the next three hours. Your discomfort is an act of allyship."

Skyler wraps his arms around himself. He is freezing. But he nods.

"Allyship," he repeats. "I am helping."

He is not helping anyone. The people without heat are still cold. Skyler is just cold with them. It is **Performative Suffering.**

But it works on him. It makes him feel like part of the Tribe. If he were warm, he would feel guilty. The Nanny State has weaponized his guilt to save a few kilowatts of power.

Finally, the lightbulb finishes updating. It turns on. It is a dim, sickly green.

Skyler checks the app. **Mode:** *Eco-Saver Night Mode.* **Brightness:** *12% (Mandatory).*

"It's better than nothing," Skyler mutters.

He sits on his couch (made of recycled plastic bottles). He eats his celery. He sits in the dim green light, shivering in his 64-degree apartment, locked out of his own refrigerator.

He owns nothing. He controls nothing. He is simply a biological component in a vast, interconnected machine that prioritizes "The Greater Good" over his immediate survival.

And the scariest part? He likes it.

He likes that he doesn't have to decide what to eat. He likes that he doesn't have to decide the temperature. He likes that the decisions are made by algorithms and bureaucrats who (he assumes) are smarter than him.

He pulls up a news article on his phone. **Title:** Why Owning Things is Outdated: The Joy of the Subscription Life.

He retweets it. "So true," he types. "Possession is just a burden."

Suddenly, his phone buzzes. A notification from the *Department of Compliance.*

"ALERT: Smart Meter data indicates a 2% increase in energy usage (The Lightbulb). This exceeds your daily carbon allowance. Your internet speed will be throttled to 3G speeds for the remainder of the evening as a penalty."

The WiFi icon on his phone drops to one bar. The video he was watching starts to buffer.

Skyler doesn't scream. He doesn't throw the phone.

He just sighs and puts the phone down. "I deserve that," he says to the empty room. "I was greedy with the light."

He curls up in the dark, under his weighted blanket, and goes to sleep.

Grok, the caveman, slept with one eye open, watching the fire he built, guarding the meat he hunted, in the cave he claimed. Grok was tired, but he was Free.

Skyler sleeps the sleep of the domesticated animal. Safe, fed (barely), and caged.

But what happens when the cage needs to be defended? The Nanny State can control the fridge, but can it control the invaders?

In the final part of this chapter, we will see Skyler face the ultimate realization: The Nanny State is great at punishing *him*, but terrible at protecting him from actual danger.

The Dial Tone of Destiny

It is 3:00 AM. The Witching Hour. The hour when Grok would have been most alert, listening for the snap of a twig that signaled a saber-tooth tiger.

Skyler is awoken not by a twig, but by a crash. A real crash. Not the "I dropped my water bottle" crash, but the sound of something heavy and burning impacting the pavement below.

He scrambles out from under his weighted blanket. He crawls to the window (avoiding the spot where the garbage bag is still flapping, lest he incur another fine). He peers out.

The street below, usually a quiet avenue of overpriced coffee shops and yoga studios, has transformed. A group of "Spirited Youth" are engaged in a "Late-Night Community Redistribution Event."

In common parlance: It is a riot.

A dumpster has been pushed into the middle of the intersection and set on fire. The flames lick the sky, casting a chaotic orange glow on the Tesla dealerships. Windows are being smashed. Merchandise is being liberated.

Skyler's heart slams against his ribs. This is danger. Real, visceral danger.

His first instinct, honed by a decade of liberal arts education, is to reframe the narrative.

They aren't rioters, he tells himself, his teeth chattering. They are the Unheard Voices of the Proletariat. That fire is a cry for help. That brick through the Starbucks window is a manifesto against corporate hegemony.

But then, a brick flies toward *his* building. It smashes the glass of the lobby door downstairs.

The narrative collapses. Skyler is scared.

He reaches for his phone. He needs the Alpha. He needs the State. He needs the men with the guns and the badges to come and restore order, so he can go back to tweeting about how bad the men with the guns and badges are.

He dials 9-1-1.

He expects immediate reassurance. He expects a calm voice saying, *"We are on the way, citizen."*

Instead, he hears a series of clicks, followed by a cheerful robotic voice.

"Thank you for calling the Department of Emergency Equity. Your call is important to us. To ensure we provide the most culturally competent response, please listen to the following menu options."

Skyler stares at the phone. "Menu? There's a fire!"

"Press 1 if you are experiencing a Mental Health Crisis and require a Conflict Mediator." "Press 2 to report a Hate Crime involving language or symbols." "Press 3 to report an environmental hazard." "Press 4 if you are witnessing a Property Dispute (formerly known as Theft/Burglary)."

Skyler presses 4 furiously.

"You have selected Property Dispute," the robot says. "Please note: In accordance with City Ordinance 45-B, property crimes under $950 are considered non-priority civil infractions. Has the value of the damaged property exceeded $950?"

"Yes!" Skyler screams at the robot. "They are burning a car!"

"Please hold while we connect you to a Community Safety Ambassador. Current wait time is... 45 minutes."

Smooth jazz begins to play.

Skyler slides down the wall. He is trapped.

The Nanny State, he realizes with a dawning horror, is incredibly efficient at the small things. It can detect a rogue lightbulb usage in seconds. It can fine him for a garbage bag via satellite imagery. It can lock his fridge remotely.

But when it comes to the big things—the things that actually threaten his life—the Nanny is on a coffee break.

The State is a micromanager who obsesses over the font size on a form but ignores the fact that the building is on fire.

Outside, the noise grows louder. Skyler hears chanting. He hears glass shattering.

He looks at his phone again. He opens the **CitizenShield** app. This is the app that replaced the police scanner.

He sees a cluster of dots on his street. **Alert:** Unsanctioned Street Party in Progress. **User Comment:** "Love the energy! The fire is so warm!" **User Comment:** "Stay safe everyone! Remember to wear masks while smashing the state!"

Skyler feels like he is living in a fever dream. No one is coming.

He remembers the "Community Safety Officers"—the unarmed social workers the city hired to replace the "aggressive" police patrol. He looks out the window.

A small Smart Car with a flashing yellow light pulls up to the burning dumpster. Two people in high-visibility vests get out. They are holding clipboards.

They approach the rioters.

"Excuse me, friends!" one of the Safety Officers yells. "We see that you are expressing some big feelings tonight! Can we offer you some pamphlets on conflict resolution?"

One of the rioters throws a flaming bottle of kombucha at the Smart Car.

The Safety Officers immediately get back in the car and drive away.

"Well," Skyler whispers. "They tried."

The police—the *actual* police—are nowhere to be seen. They are currently parked three miles away, under strict orders from the Mayor not to engage unless "lethal force is imminent," because arresting people looks bad on Instagram.

Skyler is alone.

He is locked in his Smart Cave. His fridge won't open. His light is dim. His window is broken. And the barbarians are at the gate.

He realizes he has absolutely no way to defend himself. He gave up his right to bear arms. He gave up his right to self-defense (the karate class only taught him to go limp). He gave up his agency to the State.

And the State has left him on hold.

Click.

The music stops. A human voice comes on the line.

"911, this is Dispatcher Ash. What are your pronouns?"

"He/Him!" Skyler screams. "There is a riot outside my apartment! They are burning things!"

"Sir," Ash says, their voice dripping with condescension. "Please watch your tone. We don't use the 'R' word. It is a Civil Unrest Event. Are you currently in physical danger?"

"They are throwing bricks!"

"Are they throwing bricks *at* you? Or just in your general vicinity?"

"I... I don't know! One hit the door!"

"Okay. We will log the report. Officers are currently staging at a safe distance to allow the community to vent. Please stay inside, lock your doors, and stay away from windows. Do not engage the demonstrators. Engaging creates conflict."

"So you're not coming?"

"We are monitoring the situation via drone. Have a safe night."

The line goes dead.

Skyler crawls back to his bed. He pulls the weighted blanket over his head.

He lies there, listening to the destruction of his neighborhood.

Grok, his ancestor, would be sharpening a spear right now. Grok would be standing at the entrance of the cave, ready to fight for his life. Grok would be free.

Skyler is a prisoner.

But as the adrenaline fades, a strange calm washes over him. The conditioning kicks in. The Stockholm Syndrome of the modern liberal takes the wheel.

Maybe the dispatcher is right, Skyler thinks. Who am I to police their anger? Property is theft, anyway. If they burn the building, it's just insurance money. I am safe under my blanket.

He closes his eyes.

He has been failed by every system he worships. The Technology failed. The Bureaucracy failed. The Ideology failed.

But Skyler cannot admit that. Because if he admits that, he has to admit that he is responsible for his own survival. And that is a burden too heavy to bear.

So he lies in the dark, shivering, hungry, and defenseless, and whispers the only prayer he knows:

"At least I didn't vote for the other guy."

Chapter 8
While the Romans Burned, The Liberals Tweeted

The Bridge to Nowhere (But It Has a Nice Name)

Rome did not fall in a day. It was a slow, agonizing slide into irrelevance, fueled by corruption, debauchery, and lead pipes. But at least the Romans had the excuse of lead poisoning.

The modern liberal has no such excuse. Their brain damage is entirely self-inflicted, the result of overdosing on Twitter threads and undergraduate sociology textbooks.

To witness the fall of the American Empire in real-time, we return to the City of San Francisco-adjacent (a spiritual location more than a geographic one).

Skyler is attending an Emergency City Council Meeting.

Now, you might assume an "Emergency" meeting would be called for an actual emergency. And you would be right. The city is falling apart.

- **The Potholes:** They are no longer holes; they are subterranean caverns capable of swallowing a Honda Civic whole.

- **The Water Main:** It burst three days ago, creating an unauthorized geyser that is currently flooding the basement of the local library.

- **The Bridge:** The "Old Mill Bridge," the primary artery into the city, has been rated "Structurally Deficient" by engineers since the Bush administration. Yesterday, a piece of concrete the size of a microwave fell off and crushed a Prius.

The city is crumbling. Physics is winning. The infrastructure—the boring, concrete stuff that keeps civilization from sliding back into the Stone Age—is failing.

Skyler logs into the Zoom meeting. He is ready to fight. He is ready to demand action.

But not about the bridge.

"I call this meeting to order," says Councilwoman Lark. Lark is a woman who communicates exclusively in buzzwords. She doesn't have "ideas"; she has "frameworks for equitable reimagining."

"First item on the agenda," Lark says, adjusting her webcam to show off her extensive collection of crystals. "We need to address the crisis at the Town Square."

Skyler nods vigorously. *Finally,* he thinks. *The crisis.*

"The statue of Founder Josiah P. Whittle," Lark continues, "has been determined to be causing significant emotional harm to the community."

The bridge is dropping concrete bombs on commuters. The water main is drowning books. But the crisis is a bronze man who died in 1892.

"We have received complaints," Lark says solemnly, "that Whittle's mustache is reminiscent of a patriarchal aesthetic that excludes those who cannot grow facial hair. Furthermore, archival records show that in 1888, he once frowned at a pigeon. This indicates a speciesist bias."

Skyler types into the chat: "TEAR IT DOWN! WE ARE UNSAFE!"

Suddenly, a voice breaks in. It is an audio-only caller. It is Ron, the contractor Skyler met at the Department of Compliance.

"Hey," Ron's voice crackles. "Can we talk about the bridge? A chunk of it almost killed my dog yesterday. It's rusted through. It's gonna collapse."

The Council falls silent. The silence is not one of concern for the bridge; it is one of annoyance at the interruption.

"Sir," Councilwoman Lark says, her voice dripping with ice. "Please do not center the narrative on physical infrastructure. We are discussing *symbolic* infrastructure right now. Symbols are violence."

"Concrete is violence when it hits you in the head!" Ron yells. "Fix the damn bridge!"

"I am muting you," Lark says. "You are derailing the work of healing."

Click. Ron is silenced. The bridge remains broken.

Skyler feels a surge of righteousness. "Good," he mutters. "He doesn't get it. He thinks keeping the bridge up is more important than dismantling the systemic oppression of the statue."

Let's pause and look at the Caveman comparison.

If Grok's cave was collapsing—if the roof was shaking and rocks were falling—Grok would grab a log and prop it up. He would reinforce the structure. Survival comes first. Decorating the walls comes second.

Skyler has reversed this polarity. He believes that if he paints the walls with the correct slogans, the roof will magically stop falling. He believes that **Semantics supersede Structural Engineering.**

The Council spends the next three hours debating what to replace the statue with.

- **Proposal A:** An abstract shape representing "The Void." (Rejected: Too nihilistic).
- **Proposal B:** A statue of a generic "Community Member" holding a recycling bin. (Rejected: Recycling implies consumption).
- **Proposal C:** A plaque apologizing for the fact that there used to be a statue there.

They settle on Proposal C. Cost: $450,000. Budget for bridge repair: $0.

"This is a historic victory," Skyler tweets. "We have removed the toxic gaze of Whittle. The square is safe again."

He feels accomplished. He has "done the work."

Meanwhile, outside his window, a city bus hits a pothole. The axle snaps. The bus careens into a fire hydrant. Water sprays everywhere.

Skyler hears the crash. He looks out.

"Wow," he says. "Someone should really do something about that."

He assumes "someone" is the Government. He forgets that he just watched the Government spend three hours debating a mustache.

He closes the blinds. He goes back to Twitter.

He sees a thread about how the term "Pothole" is problematic because it implies that holes are negative spaces, rather than opportunities for earth-reclamation.

"Interesting point," Skyler muses. "Maybe we shouldn't fill them. Maybe we should honor them."

He retweets it.

This is the **Nero Complex** of the modern liberal. Nero fiddled while Rome burned not because he didn't care about the fire, but because he thought his song was more important than the water buckets.

Skyler thinks his tweets are more important than the asphalt. He believes that by controlling the language, he controls reality.

But reality is a stubborn thing. Asphalt doesn't care about your pronouns. Rust doesn't care about your land acknowledgment. Gravity doesn't care about your "lived experience."

And while Skyler and the Council are busy purifying the city of its historical sins, the physical city is rotting beneath their feet.

The meeting ends. Councilwoman Lark smiles. "We did good today, everyone. We made this space inclusive."

"Inclusive," Skyler whispers, looking at his cracked ceiling (which he hasn't fixed because he's waiting for a permit). "Yes. We are winning."

Just then, the lights flicker.

The water main leak has reached the substation. The power grid is failing.

"Oh no," Skyler says. "My battery is at 12%."

He doesn't worry about the food in the fridge. He doesn't worry about the heat. He worries about the Tweet he was about to send.

Priorities.

The Potemkin Village of Paint

Having secured the moral victory of removing the "problematic" statue, Skyler feels energized. The city might be crumbling, but its *vibes* are improving, and in the digital economy, vibes are the only currency that matters.

Skyler decides to walk to his favorite co-working space, *The Huddle*. Since his electric car is uncharged (due to the solidarity blackout) and the bus is broken (due to the pothole incident), walking is his only option.

This walk requires him to navigate "The Zone."

In a functional civilization, a downtown district is a place of commerce and cleanliness. In Skyler's city, it looks like the set of a post-apocalyptic movie, but with better graphic design.

Skyler steps onto the sidewalk. Immediately, he is confronted with the physical reality of the decline.

- **The Smell:** A pungent bouquet of urine, marijuana, and artisanal despair.

- **The Obstacles:** A labyrinth of tents, shopping carts, and discarded scooters.

- **The Wildlife:** Rats the size of terriers that no longer fear humans because the City Council granted them "rodent rights" (extermination is now considered "interspecies genocide").

Grok, the caveman, would see this environment and instinctively know: *This is a bad place. I should leave or sanitize it.*

Skyler sees it and thinks: This is a vibrant tapestry of urban living.

He steps gingerly over a pile of used needles. He does not recoil in horror. He reframes the narrative. Those aren't biohazards, he tells himself. Those are evidence of a community struggling with trauma. To clean them up would be to erase the visibility of that struggle.

He leaves the needles there. He is a good ally.

He arrives at Main Street. Here, a massive city project is underway.

Skyler's heart swells. *Finally,* he thinks. *Infrastructure investment.*

He expects to see bulldozers filling the crater-sized potholes. He expects to see engineers reinforcing the crumbling facades of the buildings.

Instead, he sees a team of artists.

They are not fixing the road. They are painting the road.

The city has allocated $2.5 million for a project called **"The Asphalt of Affirmation."** The goal is to paint a massive, block-long mural directly onto the street. The mural depicts diverse hands holding diverse vegetables, surrounded by words like *BELONGING, KINETIC, and DECOLONIZE.*

Skyler watches as an artist carefully paints a bright yellow sunflower over a pothole that is three feet deep.

The pothole is not filled. It is simply camouflaged.

A car drives by. The driver, distracted by the radiant beauty of the sunflower, hits the pothole. *CRUNCH.* The car's suspension shatters. The tire explodes.

Skyler gasps. But he does not blame the hole. He blames the driver. "He didn't respect the art," Skyler mutters. "He drove right over the symbol of Belonging. Typical toxic aggression."

He takes a picture of the mural. He crops out the wrecked car and the angry driver. He applies a filter that makes the colors pop.

He tweets: "So beautiful to see my city investing in what really matters. Roads get you from A to B, but Art gets you from Ignorance to Enlightenment. #CityLife #MuralMagic"

He hits send. He feels warm inside.

He walks further down the street. He passes a storefront that used to be a pharmacy. It is now boarded up. Plywood covers the windows.

But wait! It's not just plywood. It's *curated* plywood.

The city has hired a "Blight Mitigation Consultant." Instead of solving the crime wave that caused the pharmacy to flee, they have paid artists to paint happy faces on the plywood.

One board says: *COMMUNITY.* Another says: *HOPE.* A third says: *THIS SPACE IS RESTING.*

"Resting," Skyler reads. "I love that. It's not abandoned. It's taking a mental health break."

He creates a narrative where the pharmacy didn't close because of shoplifting, but because it decided to ascend to a higher plane of non-commercial existence.

He stops at a bodega to buy a water. The price is $8.00. Skyler flinches. "$8.00?"

The clerk, a man who looks exhausted, points to a sign. **"Supply Chain Equity Surcharge: +15%."**

"It's the new tax," the clerk grunts. "To offset the carbon footprint of the delivery truck."

Skyler nods. He pays the $8.00. I am paying for the planet, he tells himself. Cheap water is a relic of the extractive economy.

As he exits the shop, a man runs past him, clutching a handful of stolen candy bars. The clerk doesn't chase him. The clerk just sighs and marks a tally sheet on the counter.

Skyler looks at the thief. He wants to say something. But then he remembers his training. *Who am I to judge his need for sugar?* Skyler thinks. *Maybe he has low blood sugar. Maybe this is a medical emergency.*

Skyler watches the thief trip over the newly painted "Asphalt of Affirmation" mural. The thief falls into the sunflower pothole.

Skyler rushes over. Not to help catch the thief, but to check the paint. "Careful!" Skyler yells. "You're scuffing the inclusivity!"

The thief scrambles out of the hole and runs away. The sunflower is ruined. A tire track and a shoe print mar the beautiful yellow paint.

Skyler is devastated. This is the real tragedy of the day. Not the theft. Not the broken car. Not the $8 water. The tragedy is that the symbol has been tarnished.

He pulls out his phone. He needs to report this. He opens the city's app.

Menu:

- *Report a Pothole (Current Wait Time: 4 Years)*
- *Report a Crime (Current Wait Time: Indefinite)*
- *Report a Micro-Aggression against Public Art (Priority Line)*

He selects the Priority Line.

"Hello," Skyler says into the voice memo. "Someone has defaced the sunflower. It feels very violent. The pothole is now visible again, and it looks ugly. Please send a restoration team immediately. My eyes are hurting."

He submits the report.

Within minutes, he receives a notification. "Thank you, Citizen. An Art Response Team has been dispatched. Estimated arrival: 10 minutes."

Skyler smiles. The system works.

The roads are broken. The businesses are closed. The crime is rampant. The water is unaffordable. But the paint? The paint will be fresh.

Skyler stands guard over the pothole, warning cars to drive around the "trauma site." He feels like a hero. He is protecting the illusion. And in the end, isn't the illusion more comfortable than the reality?

Rome is burning, yes. But Skyler is making sure the flames are at least color-coordinated.

The Livestream of the Collapse

The "Art Response Team" arrives in record time. They pull up in a pristine, solar-powered Sprinter van wrapped in a vinyl graphic that says *HEALING HUES: Emergency Aesthetics Unit.*

Four people jump out. They are not wearing hard hats or safety vests. They are wearing color-blocked jumpsuits and carrying artisanal paintbrushes made from sustainably harvested bamboo.

"Stand back!" the lead artist shouts, rushing toward the sunflower pothole. "Give the pigment room to breathe!"

They set up a perimeter. Not with caution tape, which is aggressive, but with velvet ropes. They ignore the car with the shattered axle sitting ten feet away. They ignore the driver, who is weeping into his steering wheel.

"The yellow is compromised," one artist whispers, examining the tire mark on the mural. "It's a smudge of violence."

"We need to perform a chromatic intervention," the leader says. "Bring me the Ochre of Optimism."

Skyler watches, mesmerized. This is government in action. This is tax dollars at work. It is beautiful.

Suddenly, a low rumble begins to vibrate through the soles of Skyler's vegan sneakers.

It is not a truck. It is not an earthquake. It is a structural failure.

Three blocks away, the Old Mill Bridge—the one Ron the contractor tried to warn the City Council about—finally gives up the ghost. The rust eats the last rivet. The concrete sighs.

CRACK-BOOM.

The sound is deafening. A massive section of the bridge detaches and plunges into the river below, taking a delivery truck and two electric scooters with it.

A plume of dust rises into the air, blotting out the sun. Car alarms go off. People scream.

In the Paleolithic era, this sound would trigger a survival response. *Run away. Find high ground. Help the tribe.*

Skyler does none of these things.

Skyler reaches into his pocket. He pulls out his phone. He swipes to his camera.

He hits "GO LIVE."

"Hey guys," Skyler shouts into the phone, holding it at a high angle to capture his jawline and the disaster simultaneously. "Skyler here. You are not going to believe what is happening. The bridge just... decided to deconstruct itself."

He begins to walk toward the disaster. He is drawn to it like a moth to a flame, or an influencer to a ring light.

He reaches the edge of the river. The scene is chaotic. Sirens are wailing (in the distance). People are pointing.

Skyler reads the chat as it scrolls up his screen.

- **User1:** *OMG are you okay??*
- **User2:** *That dust cloud looks kinda toxic but also aesthetic?*
- **User3:** *Is this a protest?*

"I don't know if it's a protest," Skyler narrates, panning the camera over the wreckage. "But it feels very symbolic. That bridge was built in the 1950s. It was a relic of the industrial age. Maybe... maybe it *chose* to fall? Maybe it was tired of carrying the weight of capitalism?"

A man stumbles up the riverbank. He is wet, muddy, and coughing. It is the delivery driver.

"Help!" the man wheezes. "My phone... I need to call my wife."

Skyler turns the camera on the man.

"Sir!" Skyler shouts. "You just survived the collapse! Can you tell my followers how you're processing this trauma right now? What is your emotional state?"

The man looks at the phone. He looks at Skyler. "I need a doctor!"

"He needs a doctor," Skyler repeats to the livestream. "We need universal healthcare, folks. This is proof. If we had Medicare for All, this bridge wouldn't have fallen. Wait, that doesn't make sense. But you know what I mean. Smash the like button if you agree!"

The man pushes past Skyler and limps toward a paramedic who has finally arrived.

Skyler is annoyed. Rude, he thinks. He walked right out of the frame.

He looks at his viewer count. **12,000 watching.**

The dopamine hits him hard. This is the most attention he has ever received. The city is broken, people are hurt, the infrastructure is in ruins... and Skyler is having the best day of his life.

He spots a piece of rebar sticking out of the rubble. It is twisted and gnarly.

"Look at this," Skyler whispers, zooming in. "It's like modern art. It represents the twisting of our souls under the patriarchy."

He takes a screenshot. He posts it to Instagram with the caption: *Broken, but still beautiful. #BridgeCollapse #Vibes #MondayMood.*

Within seconds, the likes pour in.

Meanwhile, behind him, the Art Response Team has finished repainting the pothole. The sunflower is bright yellow again. The velvet ropes are removed.

The lead artist looks at the bridge collapse in the distance. He shrugs. "Not my department," he says. "I do floors, not structures."

They get back in their van and drive away, carefully navigating around the emergency vehicles.

Skyler stays by the river until his battery hits 1%. He has milked the disaster for every ounce of engagement. He has turned a tragedy into content. He has successfully converted human suffering into digital clout.

As the sun sets, casting a red glow over the dust-choked city, Skyler walks home.

He has to take the long way because the bridge is gone. It takes him an extra hour. His feet hurt. He is hungry.

But he looks at his phone. The notification badge says **99+**.

He smiles.

Rome didn't fall because of barbarians. Rome fell because the citizens were too busy live-tweeting the barbarians to lock the gate.

Skyler unlocks his apartment door. He steps inside.

"Honey, I'm home!" he yells to no one.

He sits on his couch. He plugs in his phone. He watches the replay of his own livestream.

"I looked good," he murmurs. "The dust really gave me a filter effect."

He goes to sleep, dreaming of the next disaster. Maybe the library will flood? Maybe a sinkhole?

Whatever it is, he will be ready. Not with a rope, or a shovel, or a first aid kit. But with a ring light and a hashtag.

And thus, the civilization ends. Not with a bang, but with a *Send Tweet.*

Chapter 9
Biology Deniers

The Gray Cake of Ambiguity

Biology is the hardware of existence. It is the code that runs the machine. It dictates that you need oxygen to breathe, that gravity will break your leg if you jump off a cliff, and that—historically speaking—it takes a male and a female of a mammalian species to create a new version of that species.

Grok, the caveman, was a master biologist. He didn't have a degree, but he had eyes. He knew that the bull moose was the one with the antlers and the bad attitude. He knew that the cow moose was the one protecting the calf. If Grok approached a bull moose and tried to milk it, Grok died.

Lesson learned: Biology is real.

Skyler, however, has transcended biology. He believes that biology is not hardware; it is software. And like all software, he believes it can be hacked, patched, or deleted entirely if the user interface is offensive.

It is Saturday afternoon. Skyler is attending a very important social function. In the old days, this would have been called a "Baby Shower."

However, the term "Baby Shower" has been deemed problematic. "Shower" implies a cleansing, which suggests the baby is dirty. And "Baby" implies a state of infancy, which is ageist.

So, Skyler is attending a "Gestational Arrival Launch Party."

The host is his friend Jordan. Jordan is pregnant. Jordan refers to themself as a "Birthing Vessel."

Skyler arrives at the party holding a gift. Buying a gift was a nightmare. He couldn't buy blue clothes (imposing a stereotype). He couldn't buy pink clothes (imposing a construct). He couldn't buy a truck (toxic masculinity). He couldn't buy a doll (enforcing domestic servitude).

He settled on a wooden block. It is unpainted. It is square. It represents nothing. It is the perfect gift.

"Hi, Jordan!" Skyler chirps, placing the block on the 'Gift Altar.' "You look... glowing! Your vessel is radiating energy!"

"Thanks," Jordan says, rubbing their stomach. "It's been a journey. I'm just trying to listen to the fetus and let *it* tell *me* who it is."

"So true," Skyler nods. "Have you... you know... checked the... ultrasound?"

He whispers the word "ultrasound" like it's a dirty secret.

"We did," Jordan says. "The doctor tried to assign a sex at the scan. He said, 'It's a boy!' We filed a complaint immediately."

"Good for you," Skyler says. "The audacity of that doctor. Trying to box a celestial soul into a binary before it can even speak."

"Exactly," Jordan says. "We aren't doing a Gender Reveal. We are doing a **Possibility Reveal**."

The guests gather around the table. In the center sits a cake.

In a traditional (barbaric) society, the cake would be cut open to reveal Blue or Pink sponge. The tribe would cheer, knowing that the lineage would continue.

Jordan raises the knife. "Friends! We gather here not to label, but to liberate! We cut this cake to symbolize the infinite spectrum of this child's future!"

Jordan slices the cake. A hush falls over the room.

Jordan pulls out a slice.

The inside of the cake is... **Gray**.

"Gray!" the crowd cheers. "Hooray for ambiguity!"

"It is the color of potential!" Skyler shouts, clapping. "It is the color of the fog of truth!"

Skyler eats a piece of the gray cake. It tastes like vanilla and cognitive dissonance.

He feels proud. By refusing to acknowledge the physical reality of the child—who definitely has a specific set of chromosomes rapidly dividing at this very moment—they have saved it from the "violence" of being a boy or a girl.

Skyler wanders over to the children's play area. Jordan's older child, a toddler named Leaf, is playing.

Leaf is wearing a beige sack-dress. Leaf picks up a truck. Leaf says, "Vroom vroom! Crash!"

Skyler frowns. Oh no, he thinks. Leaf is performing masculine aggression.

Skyler kneels down. "Hi, Leaf. That's a nice... transport vehicle. But remember, trucks are for carrying community gardens, not for crashing."

Leaf looks at Skyler. Leaf picks up a doll. Skyler smiles. *Better.*

Leaf uses the doll to smash the truck. "Die, truck! Die!" Leaf screams.

Skyler recoils. Biology is breaking through the conditioning. The testosterone is leaking out.

He stands up, shaken. He needs to find an adult to process this with.

He finds a guest named Alex. Alex is wearing a t-shirt that says *Biology is a Social Construct*.

"The kids are so wild," Skyler laughs nervously. "It's amazing how hard we have to work to deprogram them."

"It's the water," Alex says darkly. "The micro-plastics mimic hormones. That's why that child smashed the truck. It's environmental toxicity forcing him into a predator role."

"Right," Skyler agrees. "It couldn't possibly be that boys like smashing things. That would imply... nature."

"Nature is a myth," Alex declares. "Everything is nurture. If we raised that child in a white room with no objects, he would be a perfect, genderless angel."

Skyler nods. He imagines a world of white rooms and gray cakes. It sounds peaceful. It sounds boring. But mostly, it sounds safe.

Suddenly, Jordan gasps.

"Oh!" Jordan grabs the table. "I think... I think the launch is commencing!"

"The launch?" Skyler asks.

"The water broke!" someone yells.

Panic ensues.

"Call an Uber!" Skyler yells. "We need to get to the Birth Center!"

"No!" Jordan screams. "Not the hospital! They will try to assign it! They will put a hat on it! A blue hat!"

"We have to go!" Skyler insists.

They rush Jordan to the car. Skyler drives. He is hyperventilating. He is about to witness a biological event. He is terrified.

He has spent his whole life denying that biology dictates anything. He believes that strength, pain, and hormones are just "mindsets."

But as Jordan screams in the back seat—a primal, gutteral scream that echoes back to the very first woman in the very first cave—Skyler realizes something terrifying.

This isn't a theory. This isn't a tweet. This is a mammalian body doing exactly what it was designed to do, regardless of what pronouns it uses.

"Breathe!" Skyler yells. "Visualize a non-binary geometric shape expanding!"

"SHUT UP!" Jordan roars. "GET THIS THING OUT OF ME!"

Skyler grips the wheel. The gray cake churns in his stomach. Reality is coming. And it doesn't care about the party theme.

The Triage of Truth

Skyler bursts through the automatic doors of the Emergency Room, pushing Jordan in a wheelchair. Jordan is breathing like a steam engine and gripping the armrests with enough force to crush walnuts.

"Help!" Skyler yells. "We have a gestational emergency! The cargo is breaching the hull!"

A Triage Nurse looks up from behind a plexiglass barrier. She is a woman in her sixties. She has seen everything. She has seen motorcycle accidents, overdoses, and kids with Legos stuck up their noses. She has no time for Skyler's vocabulary.

"Name?" the nurse barks, fingers hovering over a keyboard.

"Jordan," Skyler says breathless.

"Sex?"

Skyler freezes. The question hangs in the air like a foul odor.

"Excuse me?" Skyler says, straightening his posture. "That is an incredibly invasive and irrelevant question. Jordan identifies as non-binary femme-adjacent with flux tendencies."

The nurse stops typing. She peers over her glasses.

"Does the patient have a uterus?" she asks, her voice flat.

"Jordan has *internal reproductive architecture*," Skyler corrects her. "But defining it by its reproductive capacity is reductive."

"Sir," the nurse says, "if they have a uterus, they go to Labor and Delivery. If they have a prostate, they go to Urology. I need to know where to send the wheelchair."

"Biology is a spectrum!" Skyler insists, waving his hands. "You are forcing a binary choice on a quantum existence!"

"I am forcing a destination on an elevator," the nurse snaps. "Is there a baby coming out of a vagina? Yes or No?"

Skyler gasps. The word "vagina" feels like a slap in the face. It is so anatomical. So... specific.

"Yes," Jordan groans from the chair. "YES! JUST GO!"

The biology has spoken. The ideology has been overruled by the contractions.

They are whisked up to the Labor and Delivery ward. The room is white, sterile, and full of machines that go *ping*.

A doctor enters. Let's call him Dr. Stone. Dr. Stone is not an "ally." Dr. Stone is a mechanic of the human body. He deals in blood, fluid, and tissue.

"Alright," Dr. Stone says, snapping on latex gloves. "Let's take a look. Dilation check."

Skyler intervenes. He steps in front of the stirrups.

"Wait," Skyler says, holding up a hand. "Before you interact with the pelvic region, have you checked your privilege? We want this birth to be a collaborative experience. We don't want you to 'deliver' the baby. We want you to 'facilitate the transition of the entity.'"

Dr. Stone blinks. "I'm going to catch the baby so it doesn't hit the floor. Now move."

Dr. Stone checks Jordan.

"Ten centimeters," Dr. Stone says. "It's go time. Jordan, on the next contraction, I need you to push."

"Pushing is violent language!" Skyler offers helpfully from the head of the bed. "Jordan, visualize *releasing*. Visualize the child flowing out like a river."

Jordan turns to look at Skyler. Jordan's face is red, sweaty, and contorted in a mask of primal agony.

"SHUT UP, SKYLER!" Jordan roars. "I AM PUSHING!"

Skyler shrinks back. He is witnessing the collapse of the narrative.

In the wild, when a female is giving birth, the tribe protects her. They understand that this is the most dangerous and powerful moment in a human life. It is blood and pain and life. It is raw.

Skyler is trying to sanitize it. He is trying to put a "Content Warning" on a biological function.

"Okay, here we go," Dr. Stone says. "I see the head."

"Don't assign a head!" Skyler whispers. "It's a cranial possibility."

"Big push!" Dr. Stone commands.

Jordan pushes. The room fills with the sound of effort. It is a sound that has echoed in caves, in huts, and in hospitals for a million years. It is the sound of the species surviving.

And then, with a wet squelch and a cry, the baby arrives.

Dr. Stone lifts the infant into the air. The baby is red, squalling, and covered in vernix. It is a messy, beautiful, undeniable chunk of reality.

"It's a boy!" Dr. Stone announces cheerfully.

Skyler screams.

"NO!" Skyler yells. "Don't say that! You'll imprint him! I mean... them! You have violated their consent! They haven't declared their pronouns yet!"

Dr. Stone ignores Skyler. He places the baby on Jordan's chest.

"He's a healthy baby boy," Dr. Stone says gently to the mother. "Look at him."

Jordan looks down. The ideology, for a brief, shimmering moment, dissolves.

Jordan doesn't see a "genderless entity." Jordan doesn't see a "social construct." Jordan sees a son.

"He's beautiful," Jordan whispers, tears streaming down their face. "My boy."

Skyler is hyperventilating in the corner. He feels like he has failed. The doctor used the B-word (Boy). The mother accepted it. The gray cake was a lie. The baby clearly has the hardware of a male.

This is a disaster, Skyler thinks. We have already started the indoctrination.

He approaches the bed cautiously.

"Jordan," he whispers. "I know you're emotional right now. The hormones—which are valid—are clouding your judgment. But let's not rush to labels. Let's call the baby 'X' for now."

Jordan looks at Skyler with the eyes of a mother wolf who is considering eating a particularly annoying coyote.

"His name is Liam," Jordan says firmly.

"Liam?" Skyler gasps. "That's... that's a traditionally masculine name! What about 'River'? What about 'Sage'? What about 'Brick'?"

"Liam," Jordan repeats. "And he's hungry."

Jordan begins to breastfeed.

Skyler's brain short-circuits.

Breastfeeding.

He knows this is "natural," but it feels so... traditional. It implies that the body has a specific function. It implies that the biology of the mother is designed to nurture the biology of the child.

It implies that **Nature has a Plan**.

And if Nature has a plan, then Skyler's entire worldview—that we can invent our own reality—is wrong.

If milk is made for the baby, and the baby is made for the milk, then the universe is not a blank slate. It is a structured system.

Skyler cannot handle this. He needs to retreat to the digital world, where he can block Nature.

He pulls out his phone. He takes a picture of the baby's foot (the only part he deems gender-neutral enough to post).

He types a caption: "The Entity has arrived. The doctor was very aggressive with labels (creating trauma), but we are holding space for this little human to tell us who they are. Welcome to the world, X. #Newborn #NoGender #SmashTheBinary"

He posts it.

Then, he looks at the comments.

Comment 1: Awww! Is it a boy or a girl?

Skyler's thumb hovers over the block button.

Why does everyone care? he thinks furiously. Why is biology the first thing they ask about?

Because, Skyler, deep down, even the most conditioned human knows that the first rule of survival is knowing what you are.

Grok knew it. The Doctor knows it. Even Jordan, in the exhaustion of birth, knows it.

Only Skyler, the modern intellectual, remains in the dark.

He puts his phone away. He looks at Liam. Liam is crying. It is a loud, demanding cry.

"He has a strong set of lungs," Dr. Stone says, washing his hands. "He's going to be a linebacker."

Skyler shudders. "Linebacker" implies contact sports. Contact sports imply competition. Competition implies winners and losers.

"Or," Skyler suggests weakly, "he could be a... a very loud librarian."

Dr. Stone laughs. It is a hearty, biological laugh.

"Sure, buddy. Whatever you say."

Dr. Stone leaves the room to go deliver another dose of reality to another family.

Skyler is left alone with the mother and child. The room is quiet now. The reality of life is heavy in the air.

Skyler feels small. He feels like a ghost trying to haunt a house that is full of living, breathing people. He realizes, with a sinking feeling, that no matter how many words he invents, he cannot tweet away a chromosome.

But he will try. Oh, he will try.

In Part 3, we will see Skyler attempt to raise a child (or rather, give unsolicited advice on raising a child) in a world that refuses to play along with his fantasy. We will visit the "Gender-Neutral Playground."

The Sandbox of Sameness

Fast forward three years. Skyler is now the designated "Community Guardian" (babysitter) for little Liam.

Jordan needs a break to attend a "Scream Therapy Retreat," so Skyler has volunteered to take Liam to the park. But not just any park. They are going to the **Unity play-scape**.

In the Paleolithic era, "play" was practice for survival. Children chased each other (hunting practice). Children wrestled (combat practice). Children climbed trees (escape practice). If a child fell out of a tree, they learned a valuable lesson about gravity. If they poked themselves with a sharp stick, they learned about physics.

The Unity Play-scape, however, has been designed by a committee of liability lawyers and child psychologists who believe that "risk" is a form of trauma.

There are no swings. (Swings promote kinetic inequality; some kids go higher than others). There is no merry-go-round. (Centrifugal force is ableist). There is no jungle gym. (Height creates hierarchy).

Instead, the park consists of several large, foam blobs painted in soothing shades of beige and taupe. The ground is made of recycled rubber that is six inches thick, ensuring that even if a child were to dive headfirst from a standing position, they would simply bounce.

Skyler leads Liam to the "Zone of Reflection."

"Okay, Liam," Skyler says. "Go play. But remember: No running (it's aggressive), no shouting (it disturbs the peace), and if you interact with another child, ask for their pronouns first."

Liam, a three-year-old with the energy of a nuclear reactor, looks at the beige blob. He looks at Skyler. He looks at a pile of mulch.

Liam runs to the mulch.

"Liam! No!" Skyler chides. "The mulch is for aesthetic grounding, not for engagement!"

Liam ignores him. He digs in the dirt. He finds a stick.

It is a good stick. It is roughly L-shaped. It has a handle and a barrel.

Skyler watches in horror. He knows what is coming. It is the genetic memory of a thousand generations of hunters.

Liam raises the stick. He points it at a squirrel.

"Pew! Pew!" Liam shouts.

Skyler sprints across the rubber safety surface. "Liam! Drop the weapon!"

He snatches the stick from the toddler. Liam bursts into tears.

"We do not use sticks as guns," Skyler lectures, crouching down. "Guns are tools of the patriarchy. This stick is... a wand! A wand of kindness! Look!"

Skyler waves the stick gently. "Swish, swish! I am spreading glitter and equity!"

Liam stops crying. He looks at the stick. He grabs it back.

"Flamethrower!" Liam yells, making a *whoosh* sound.

Skyler gasps. *Flamethrower? Where did he even learn that word?* They don't have a TV. They only read books about gender-neutral bears who share honey.

It is intrinsic. It is the Boy Code.

Skyler looks around. He sees he is losing control of the narrative. Across the playground, a group of children—mostly boys, but a few tomboys—have gathered. They have found more sticks. They are forming a militia.

"We take the hill!" one boy screams.

The "hill" is a slightly elevated beige mound.

"Charge!" the others yell.

They run. They shout. They are aggressive. They are loud. They are having the time of their lives.

Skyler feels the need to intervene. This is Toxic Masculinity in its larval stage. If he doesn't stop it now, these boys will grow up to be... well, functional men who can defend things. And Skyler can't have that.

He marches over to the militia.

"Excuse me, friends!" Skyler uses his 'Teacher Voice.' "Let's pause. Let's create a circle. Why are we fighting? Can't we use our words to negotiate access to the beige mound?"

The General of the army—a four-year-old missing a front tooth—looks at Skyler.

"You're dead," the General says, pointing a stick at Skyler. "Laser blast."

"I am not dead," Skyler argues. "I am a non-combatant peacekeeper."

"You're a zombie," the General corrects himself. "Zombies eat brains. Get him!"

The unit turns. Ten children with sticks advance on Skyler.

Skyler feels a genuine pang of fear. These are small humans, but they are feral. They are tapping into a biological software that Skyler has uninstalled. They are unified. They have a mission. And they have weapons.

"Now, now," Skyler backs away. "Let's use our 'Safe Hands'..."

"Get the zombie!" they scream.

Skyler turns and runs. He runs across the rubber matting. He runs past the "Zone of Reflection." He runs past the other parents, who are too busy scrolling on their phones to notice that the *Lord of the Flies* is re-enacting itself ten feet away.

He grabs Liam (who is currently trying to gnaw on the beige blob) and flees the park.

"We are leaving, Liam!" Skyler pants. "That space was not safe. It was full of unregulated testosterone."

"I want the stick!" Liam wails.

"No sticks!" Skyler snaps. "From now on, we only play with soft cubes."

They get into the car. Skyler buckles Liam in. He leans his head against the steering wheel.

He is exhausted. He is fighting a war against Nature, and Nature is kicking his butt.

He realizes, deep down, that you can paint the nursery gray, you can ban the toy guns, and you can lecture the toddlers about equity... but you cannot police the DNA.

The boys wanted to conquer the hill. The girls (who were huddled in a corner of the playground) were busy creating a complex social hierarchy involving the trade of acorns. The biology was asserting itself.

Skyler starts the car. He feels defeated.

"Why is it so hard?" he whispers to himself. "Why won't they just be... neutral?"

Because, Skyler, survival isn't neutral. Survival is active. Survival is aggressive. Survival is a team sport played with sharp sticks.

And as Skyler drives away, heading back to his safe, temperature-controlled, ideologically pure apartment, he doesn't realize that the final test is coming.

He has failed at fire. He has failed at hunting. He has failed at defense. He has failed at biology.

Now, the Safety Net is about to snap. The grid is about to go down. The trucks are going to stop running.

And Skyler, the man who has spent his entire life trying to return to the womb of the State, is about to be birthed into the cold, hard world of the Caveman.

The Great Reset is here.

Chapter 10
The Great Reset (Back to Zero)

The Blue Screen of Death (Real Life Edition)

It didn't happen with a bang. It didn't happen with a nuclear flash or an alien invasion. It happened on a Tuesday, at 2:43 PM, while Skyler was in the middle of a heated Twitter thread regarding the cultural appropriation of "Taco Tuesdays" by non-Latinx cafeterias.

He was typing: "It's not just food, it's erasure. By consuming the taco without honoring the maize god, you are literally consuming a culture."

He hit **Send**.

The loading circle spun. And spun. And spun.

Then, the Wi-Fi icon on his laptop vanished. Then, the LTE bars on his phone turned to "No Service." Then, the lights hummed once, flickered, and died. Then, the low hum of the refrigerator stopped. Then, the ambient noise of the city—the distant traffic, the sirens, the construction—faded into an eerie, suffocating silence.

Skyler sat in the gloom of his apartment.

"Hello?" he said.

His voice sounded small. It didn't echo. It just fell flat on the recycled bamboo flooring.

He wasn't worried yet. Power outages happened. The grid was "equitable," which meant it was unreliable. He assumed the Department of Energy was just doing a rolling blackout to celebrate Earth Hour (which was usually in March, but maybe they moved it).

He waited.

Hour 1: Skyler eats the rest of his celery. He tries to read a physical book, but finds the lack of hyperlinks frustrating. He keeps tapping words to see the definition, but the paper refuses to interact.

Hour 3: The apartment is getting cold. The Smart Thermostat is a blank black square. Skyler wraps himself in his weighted blanket. He assumes the authorities are working on it. "They are probably dispatching the solar drones," he reassures himself.

Hour 6: The sun goes down. The city outside is pitch black. Not the "urban dark" where streetlights and office buildings cast a glow. This is *ancient* dark. This is the dark of a cave before the discovery of fire.

Skyler looks out the window. There are no lights. No cars moving. Just shadows.

He feels the first twinge of real panic. He tries to call 911. The line is dead. Not busy—*dead*. The dial tone, that comforting hum of the infrastructure, is gone.

Hour 12: Skyler is thirsty. He goes to the tap. He turns the handle. A pathetic sputtering sound. A few drops of brown water. Then, a dry hiss.

The electric pumps that push water up to the 4th floor have failed.

"Okay," Skyler whispers, his voice trembling. "This is a serious outage. I need to check the Neighborhood App."

He taps his phone. It is a brick. It has 40% battery, but without a network, it is just a flashlight that can also play Candy Crush.

He realizes he has no way to get information. He doesn't own a radio (AM/FM is for boomers). He doesn't talk to his neighbors (social anxiety). He doesn't have a landline.

He is an island. A highly educated, ideologically pure, completely helpless island.

He decides he must venture out. He needs supplies. He needs to find the "Authorities."

He dresses in his most tactical gear: Joggers, a hoodie, and his pristine hiking boots. He grabs his "Bug Out Bag." The bag contains:

- A solar charger (useless at night).
- A bag of fair-trade coffee beans (unedible).
- A copy of *The Communist Manifesto* (inedible).
- A bottle of CBD oil (for anxiety).
- A whistle (for... whistling?).

He opens his apartment door. The hallway is black. The electronic key fob system is dead, meaning the security doors at the lobby are likely unlocked. Or permanently locked.

He creeps down the stairs. The stairwell smells of fear.

He pushes open the lobby door. He steps onto the street.

The silence is broken by sounds he has never heard in the city before. The sound of breaking glass. The sound of shouting. The sound of dogs barking—not the yippy doodles of the dog park, but the deep, throaty barks of animals realizing the leash is gone.

Skyler walks toward the local Whole Foods. In his mind, Whole Foods is a sanctuary. It is a place of abundance. Surely, the Amazon Prime vans will still be running. Jeff Bezos wouldn't let the supply chain fail, right?

He arrives at the store.

The windows are smashed. The shelves are stripped.

It looks like a swarm of locusts moved through Aisle 4. The quinoa is gone. The oat milk is gone. The gluten-free crackers are gone.

Standing in the middle of the produce section, holding a bruised eggplant, is a man. He is wearing a suit, but his tie is undone. He looks like a lawyer who has lost his mind.

"Excuse me," Skyler whispers. "Is there a manager?"

The lawyer laughs. It is a manic, terrifying sound.

"The manager?" the lawyer cackles. "The manager left three hours ago. He took the last crate of probiotic yogurt and ran."

"But... who is in charge?" Skyler asks.

"Nobody," the lawyer says. "Or maybe... everybody."

The lawyer takes a bite out of the raw eggplant. He stares at Skyler.

"Do you have a weapon?" the lawyer asks.

"I have a whistle," Skyler says, holding it up. "And I know non-violent communication."

The lawyer snorts. "You're dead meat, kid. The grid is fried. Solar flare? Cyber attack? Who knows. But the trucks aren't coming. The water is off. It's Day One of the Stone Age."

Skyler backs away. "No," he says. "The government will send aid. They have stockpiles."

"The government is comprised of people like you," the lawyer says, spitting out a piece of eggplant skin. "People who sit in meetings and discuss synergy. They are currently hiding under their desks."

Skyler turns and runs.

He runs back toward his apartment. But as he turns the corner, he sees something that stops him cold.

A fire. A real fire.

In the middle of the intersection, a group of people have gathered. They are not rioting. They are cooking. They have built a fire pit out of cobblestones torn from the street. They are roasting something on a spit.

It smells delicious. It smells like survival.

Skyler approaches cautiously. He hides behind a Prius that has been abandoned in the middle of the road.

He peers at the group. It is Hank. His neighbor. The guy with the Ford F-150. The guy Skyler hated. And Ron. The contractor who wanted to fix the bridge. And Steve. The guy from the toothpaste aisle.

They are laughing. They are warm. They are armed. Hank has a shotgun leaning against his truck. Ron has a generator humming in the back of his van, powering a string of lights.

They look... comfortable.

They are the **Barbarians**. The people Skyler mocked for being "outdated." The people he called "toxic."

But looking at them now, Skyler doesn't see toxins. He sees Competence. He sees men who know how to start a fire. Men who know how to fix things. Men who have cans of beans that aren't "artisanal," but are actually edible.

Skyler looks at his whistle. He looks at his CBD oil.

He realizes, with a crushing weight of clarity, that he is not the protagonist of this story. He is not the hero who rebuilds society.

He is the NPC (Non-Player Character) who dies in the cutscene to show how dangerous the world is.

His stomach grumbles. The smell of the roasting meat (is that a squirrel? A pigeon?) is intoxicating.

He has a choice. He can go back to his cold, dark, smart apartment and tweet into the void until he starves. Or he can approach the Barbarians and beg.

He steps out from behind the Prius.

"Hello?" Skyler calls out, his voice cracking. "I... I come in peace?"

Hank turns. He squints into the darkness. He racks the slide of the shotgun. *Chunk-chunk.*

"Who goes there?" Hank booms.

"It's Skyler," Skyler squeaks. "From 4B. I... I filed a noise complaint against you last month?"

Hank lowers the gun slightly. He grins. It is the grin of a man who knows he has won the cultural war simply by surviving it.

"Well, well," Hank says. "If it isn't the Hall Monitor. You hungry, Skyler?"

"Yes," Skyler whispers. "Please."

"Come on over," Hank says. "But leave the whistle. And the attitude."

Skyler walks toward the fire. The warmth hits his face. It is the first time he has been warm in twelve hours.

He sits down on a bucket. Ron hands him a plate of beans.

"Thank you," Skyler says.

"Don't thank me," Ron says. "Thank the supply chain I stockpiled while you were busy trying to cancel Dr. Seuss."

Skyler takes a bite. It is the best thing he has ever tasted.

He looks into the fire. The flames dance. They are primal. They are real. The Blue Screen of Death has consumed the world he knew. The apps are gone. The hashtags are gone. The Safe Spaces are gone.

All that is left is the Fire, the Tribe, and the Meat.

Skyler has finally returned to the Cave. And for the first time in his life, he shuts up and eats.

The Intern of the Apocalypse

The sun rises on Day 2 of the New Stone Age.

It is a gray, dismal dawn. The air smells of smoke and uncollected garbage. Skyler wakes up curled in the fetal position on a piece of cardboard next to Hank's truck. His back hurts. His neck hurts. His pride hurts.

He sits up. His $200 tactical joggers are stained with soot. His "Bug Out Bag" looks pathetic next to Ron's military-surplus duffel.

The camp is already awake. Hank is stripping the insulation off some copper wire. Ron is siphoning gas from an abandoned sedan. Steve is sharpening a machete on a curb.

They are working. They are industrious. They are the new Aristocracy.

Skyler stands up, brushing the ash off his hoodie. He feels the urge to contribute. After all, he was a Project Manager. He knows how to lead teams (via Zoom).

"Good morning, team," Skyler says, his voice cracking slightly. "I was thinking, before we start the day's workflows, we should do a quick stand-up meeting to align on our KPIs."

Hank stops stripping wire. He looks at Skyler.

"KPIs?" Hank asks.

"Key Performance Indicators," Skyler explains, falling into his comfort zone. "We need to establish a mission statement. What is our core competency here? Is it foraging? Is it defense? We need to avoid siloed working."

Ron stops siphoning gas. He wipes his hands on a rag.

"Our core competency," Ron says slowly, "is not dying."

"Right, right," Skyler nods. "But how do we measure that? Do we have a spreadsheet? A tracker?"

"Here is the tracker," Steve says, pointing the machete at the fire pit. "If the fire is on, we are good. If the fire is off, we freeze. If the belly is empty, we starve."

Skyler frowns. "That seems a bit reductive. We should really map out the stakeholders."

Hank stands up. He towers over Skyler. Hank is a man who has eaten red meat his entire life. He is solid.

"Listen, Sunshine," Hank says. "The world you lived in? The one with the apps and the meetings and the HR complaints? That's gone. It's flushed. We are back to the basics. The basics are: Input and Output."

"I understand economics," Skyler says defensively. "I took a seminar on the post-scarcity economy."

"There is no post-scarcity," Hank says. "There is only scarcity. And right now, you are a mouth. You are an Input. We need to know if you can be an Output."

This is the Job Interview.

"What can you do?" Hank asks. "Can you weld?"

"No," Skyler says. "But I can weld... narratives?"

Hank shakes his head. "Can you hunt? Can you track a deer?"

"I... I can track a package on UPS," Skyler offers. "But I assume the servers are down."

"Can you fix an alternator?" Ron asks.

"I don't know what that is," Skyler admits.

"Can you grow food?" Steve asks. "Do you know how to plant corn?"

"I grew a succulent once," Skyler says. "His name was Bartholomew. He died of root rot."

The three men look at each other. They are calculating the caloric return on investment of keeping Skyler alive. It is not looking good.

"Okay," Hank says. "You have no skills. You have no muscle. You have no tools. But, we aren't savages. We won't leave you to the wolves. Yet."

"Thank you," Skyler breathes. "I appreciate the inclusivity."

"Don't thank me," Hank says. "You're going to work. Since you can't build, hunt, or fix... you get the jobs that require zero brain power."

Hank points to a shovel leaning against the truck.

"We need a latrine," Hank says. "Go behind that retaining wall. Dig a hole. Four feet deep. Two feet wide."

Skyler stares at the shovel. It is a tool of manual labor. It is a symbol of the working class. Skyler has always championed the working class from his laptop, but he has never actually *been* the working class.

"Digging?" Skyler asks. "Is there a... a machine? Or a contractor we can call?"

"You are the contractor," Ron grins. "Get to it. The ground is frozen, so put your back into it."

Skyler grabs the shovel. It is heavy. The handle is rough wood. It is not ergonomic.

He walks behind the retaining wall. He looks at the ground. It is hard, packed earth mixed with city gravel.

He strikes the ground with the shovel. *Clang.* It barely scratches the surface.

This is going to be hard.

Skyler hits the ground again. And again. Within five minutes, his hands are blistering. Within ten minutes, he is sweating in the freezing air. Within twenty minutes, his back is screaming.

He stops. He leans on the shovel. He pulls out his phone out of habit, wanting to tweet: *Manual labor is so validating, but also literal violence against my lumbar spine.* The phone is still dead. He has no audience. He has only the hole.

He realizes something profound: **Work is real.** All his life, "work" meant moving digital files from one folder to another. It meant sitting in a chair and talking. It meant "emotional labor," which left him tired but clean.

This is physics. This is energy transfer. And he is weak.

He looks back at the camp. Hank is building a shelter out of tarps and plywood. He moves with efficiency. He measures by eye. He cuts with confidence. Hank is an artist of survival. Skyler is a child playing in the dirt.

An hour passes. The hole is one foot deep.

Hank walks over. He looks at the hole. He looks at Skyler.

"Pathetic," Hank says. But it's not malicious. It's just an observation. "You're holding the shovel wrong. You're using your arms. Use your legs. Kick it in."

Hank grabs the shovel. He demonstrates. *Thump. Scoop. Toss. Thump. Scoop. Toss.* In thirty seconds, Hank moves more dirt than Skyler moved in an hour.

"See?" Hank hands the shovel back. "Physics doesn't care about your feelings. It cares about leverage."

Skyler nods. "Leverage," he repeats. "Right."

He gets back to work. He tries to copy Hank. It works a little better.

By noon, the hole is dug. Skyler is exhausted. He is covered in filth. He has never been this dirty in his life. He smells like sweat and earth.

He walks back to the fire. He expects a gold star. He expects a "Participation Trophy."

"I did it," Skyler announces, dropping the shovel. "The hole is dug. I have facilitated the waste management solution."

"Good," Ron says. "Now go fill these water jugs from the river. Then boil the water. Then filter it through this charcoal."

"More?" Skyler asks. "But... I did the hole. I need a break. I need to recharge my bandwidth."

"Bandwidth is for internet," Steve says. "You eat when the work is done. The water is low. Go."

Skyler wants to argue. He wants to cite labor laws. He wants to call a union rep. But then he looks at the pot over the fire. It is bubbling with a stew made from the scavenged contents of the Whole Foods dumpster. It smells like life.

If he doesn't work, he doesn't eat. The equation is absolute.

He picks up the jugs. They are heavy.

He walks to the river. As he walks, he passes other groups of survivors. He sees a group of "Tech Bros" in Patagonia vests trying to start a fire by rubbing two iPhones together (metaphorically). They are freezing. They are arguing about whose fault it is. He sees a group of "Influencers" posing in front of a smashed storefront, trying to capture the "aesthetic" of the apocalypse, even though no one can see it.

Skyler realizes he is lucky. He found the Barbarians. He found the men who know how to do things.

He fills the jugs. The water is freezing. His hands are numb. He starts the long walk back up the hill.

He is the intern. He is the grunt. He is the lowest status male in the tribe. And for the first time in his life, he has a clear purpose.

Don't drop the water.

He trudges up the hill. His muscles burn. His "Brand Narrative" is dead. His "Identity" is dead. He is just a mammal carrying heavy things to the cave.

And strangely... he doesn't hate it. Because the water is real. The weight is real. And when he gets back, the food will be real.

He enters the camp. "Water's here," he grunts.

"Good job, slick," Hank says.

Skyler sits by the fire. Hank hands him a bowl of stew. Skyler eats. He doesn't ask if it's gluten-free. He doesn't ask if the squirrel was ethically sourced.

He just eats.

"Tomorrow," Hank says, looking at the fire, "we start building the wall. We're going to need mud. Lots of mud."

Skyler nods. "I can dig mud."

"I know you can," Hank says. "You're getting better at it."

Skyler smiles. It is a dirty, tired, genuine smile.

He leans back against a tire. The stars are coming out. Without the light pollution of the city, the sky is a blanket of diamonds. It is beautiful.

Skyler realizes he never looked up before. He was always looking down at his screen.

He closes his eyes. He is sore. He is dirty. He is a servant to a bunch of guys he used to block on Twitter.

But he is alive.

And tomorrow, he has a job to do

The New Old World

Six months pass.

The seasons turn. The "Great Silence," as they call it, has settled over the city. The screaming stopped after week three. The fires stopped after month two. Now, there is only the quiet rustle of wind through the broken windows of the skyscrapers and the occasional bark of a feral dog pack hunting in the ruins of a lululemon.

We find Skyler again.

He has changed. The tactical joggers are gone, replaced by a pair of heavy canvas pants scavenged from a construction site. The alpaca wool beanie is gone, replaced by a hat made from the pelt of a raccoon that made the mistake of raiding the food stores.

Skyler has a beard. A real one. Not the manicured "stubble" he used to maintain with $40 oil, but a thick, bushy forest that protects his face from the wind. His hands, once soft enough to feel the texture of a touchscreen, are now covered in calluses thick enough to strike a match on.

He is crouching by the riverbank, scrubbing a shirt against a rock.

He is humming. It is not a protest song. It is not an indie-folk ballad. It is a simple, rhythmic tune that helps him keep time with the scrubbing.

"Input, Output," he mutters. "Clean shirt, warm body."

Hank approaches. Hank looks like a warlord from a Mad Max movie, but cleaner. He is wearing a vest made of tires (armor against the wild dogs) and carrying a spear tipped with a sharpened piece of rebar.

"Skyler," Hank grunts.

"Chief," Skyler replies. He doesn't say it ironically. Hank is the Chief. Hank kept them alive. Therefore, Hank gets the title.

"We have visitors at the perimeter," Hank says. "A group from the University District. They look... soft. I need you to translate."

Skyler stands up. He wrings out the shirt. "On it."

Skyler is the Tribe's "Diplomat." Why? Because he speaks the Old Language. He speaks *Woke*. When refugees arrive speaking in academic riddles and sociological buzzwords, Hank doesn't understand them. Skyler does.

They walk to the barricade—a wall made of overturned Teslas and concrete barriers.

Standing on the other side is a group of four people. They look ragged. They are thin. They are shivering. But they are still clinging to the remnants of their previous status. One is holding a clipboard. One is wearing a "Vote Blue" pin on a tattered sash.

"Halt," Skyler says, leaning over the hood of a Model X. "State your business."

The leader of the refugees, a man with broken glasses, steps forward.

"Greetings," the man says. "We are the 'Coalition of Sustainable Tomorrow.' We are seeking asylum. We bring intellectual capital. We are experts in critical theory, non-profit management, and digital marketing."

Hank looks at Skyler. "What did he say?"

Skyler translates: "He says they don't know how to do anything."

Hank frowns. "Do they have food?"

"We have seeds!" the refugee shouts. "Heirloom seeds!"

Hank perks up. "Seeds are good. What kind? Corn? Potatoes?"

The refugee hesitates. "Well... mostly garnish. Micro-greens. Radishes. And some artisanal lavender for calming teas."

Hank sighs. He looks at Skyler. "Tell them the rules."

Skyler nods. He looks at the refugees. He sees his former self in them. He sees the arrogance of the useless.

"Listen to me," Skyler says, his voice deep and gravelly. "We don't need digital marketing. The internet is dead. We don't need non-profit management. There is no profit. We don't need critical theory. The only theory here is: *Can you carry a log?*"

"That's ableist!" one of the refugees shrieks. "We have varying levels of physical capacity! We demand accommodation!"

Skyler laughs. It is a harsh sound.

"Nature doesn't accommodate," Skyler says. "The winter doesn't care about your back pain. The wolves don't care about your pronouns. If you want to come in, you work. You dig latrines. You haul water. You skin rats."

The refugees recoil in horror. "Skin rats? That's barbaric!"

"It's protein," Skyler says. "And it's organic."

The refugees huddle together. They whisper. Finally, the leader speaks.

"We... we choose to go elsewhere. We will find a community that values our minds."

"Good luck," Skyler says. "Head south. I hear the ruins of the Apple Store have a nice roof. But watch out for the bear. He's a Libertarian. He takes everything."

The refugees shuffle away, clutching their lavender seeds.

Hank nods at Skyler. "Good job. 'Nature doesn't accommodate.' You're getting wise, kid."

"I had a good teacher," Skyler says.

They walk back to the fire.

The camp is bustling. Steve is curing leather. Ron is building a wind turbine out of a bicycle wheel and some plastic sheeting. Children are playing—real playing, running with sticks, chasing chickens, learning to be part of the pack.

Skyler sits by the fire. He pulls something out of his pocket.

It is his old iPhone. The screen is cracked. The battery has been dead for months. It is a cold, black rectangle of glass and lithium.

He looks at it.

Six months ago, this device was his god. It told him what to think, what to eat, who to hate, and who to fear. It was his connection to the "Hive Mind."

Now, it is just a rock. A shiny, useless rock.

He remembers the fear he used to feel. The fear of being canceled. The fear of using the wrong word. The fear of the weather. The fear of the air.

He realizes he hasn't been afraid in months. He has been cold. He has been hungry. He has been tired. But he hasn't been *anxious*.

Because anxiety lives in the future, in the "what if." Survival lives in the "right now." When you are busy keeping the fire lit, you don't have time to worry about the socio-economic implications of the firewood.

He looks at the phone one last time.

"Siri," he whispers to the dead screen. "What is the meaning of life?"

The phone, obviously, says nothing.

"Wrong answer," Skyler says. "The answer is: *Keep the fire lit.*"

He stands up. He winds up his arm. He throws the iPhone into the center of the bonfire.

The plastic melts. The lithium battery hisses and pops, sending a shower of green sparks into the night sky.

"Pretty," Ron says, looking up from his work. "What was that?"

"Just some old baggage," Skyler says.

He picks up a log. He throws it on the fire. The sparks rise up, joining the stars.

The circle is complete.

Skyler started as a man who thought he was a god because he could order food with his thumb. He became a man who thought he was a victim because the world didn't obey his thumb. And finally, he became a man. Just a man. Sitting in a cave (or a retrofitted parking garage), staring at the fire, surrounded by his tribe.

He isn't progressive. He isn't conservative. He isn't a Democrat or a Republican.

He is Homo Sapiens.

He takes a deep breath of the smoky air. He looks at his dirty hands. He smiles.

"Hey Hank," Skyler yells.

"Yeah?"

"Pass the rat. I'm starving."

Hank tosses him a skewer. Skyler catches it. He takes a bite.

It tastes like victory.

The decline is over. The climb back up has begun. But this time, maybe—just maybe—they'll leave the hashtags behind.

THE END

Epilogue

A Note from the Future

Archaeologists in the year 3000 will eventually excavate the ruins of this era. They will find the plastic skeletons of the Smart Fridges. They will find the fossilized remains of the Gender-Neutral Playgrounds. They will find millions of iPhones, clutching the skeletal hands of their owners.

And they will wonder: What happened to these people? They had the power of gods. They could fly. They could speak across oceans. They split the atom.

Then, they will find a cave painting. It will be crudely drawn in charcoal on the wall of a parking structure.

It will depict a man throwing a glowing rectangle into a fire. And underneath, scrawled in primitive English, the final wisdom of the lost civilization:

"Touch Grass."

Afterword

The Road Back from the Brink

We have spent the last ten chapters laughing. We have laughed at Skyler's inability to start a fire, his terror of a pronoun, and his worship of a bureaucracy that despises him. We have laughed because satire is a mirror, and sometimes the only way to process the absurdity of the modern world is to find the humor in it.

But when the laughter fades, a terrifying question remains: **What happens when the satire becomes a documentary?**

The story of Skyler is not just a joke about a helpless liberal in a power outage. It is a warning about a civilization that has systematically severed its own roots. We are witnessing a culture that is trying to build a skyscraper starting from the penthouse down, completely ignoring the foundation upon which the structure stands.

That foundation is not technology. It is not "progress." It is not the government.

The foundation of Western Civilization—the very bedrock that allowed for the freedom, prosperity, and safety we have taken for granted—is built upon **Conservative Values** and **Christian Morality**.

For centuries, our society was guided by a set of objective truths. We believed that the family was the essential unit of society. We believed that hard work was a virtue, that personal responsibility was the price of liberty, and that there was a moral law higher than the State. We understood that "Truth" was not a personal construct to be invented, but an external reality to be discovered and obeyed.

In the last few decades, however, we have seen a deliberate erosion of these values. We have seen the secularization of our culture, where Faith is treated as a superstition and God is exiled from the public square. We have seen the destruction of the nuclear family, the demonization of masculinity, and the elevation of the "Self" to the status of a deity.

And look at the result.

We have created a generation like Skyler: morally adrift, spiritually empty, and utterly dependent on a system that views them as data points rather than souls. By removing the "restrictions" of Christian morality—the Ten Commandments, the sanctity of life, the covenant of marriage—we did not liberate ourselves. We enslaved ourselves to our own impulses and to a Nanny State that rushed in to fill the void left by the church and the father.

A society that believes in nothing will fall for anything.

We see this in the abandonment of biology for ideology. We see this in the trading of liberty for safety. We see this in the collapse of our communities, where neighbors no longer trust one another because they no longer share a common moral language.

If we want to stop the slide back to the cave—if we want to avoid the "Great Reset" where we end up shivering in the dark—we must have the courage to turn around.

Reversing this decline requires more than voting for the right candidate or lowering taxes. It requires a spiritual and cultural revival. It requires us to embrace the uncomfortable truth that **we cannot govern ourselves if we are not governed by God.**

We need to return to the values that built this nation.

- **Faith:** Acknowledging that our rights come from our Creator, not the government, and that we are accountable to Him.

- **Family:** Protecting the sanctity of the home and raising children who know who they are and what they are made for.

- **Truth:** rejecting the lie of moral relativism and standing firm on the absolutes of right and wrong.

- **Work:** Valuing the dignity of labor and the independence it brings.

The "Cave" is not just a place of physical darkness; it is a place of spiritual darkness. It is a place where man is alone, frightened, and ruled by the strongest brute or the loudest demagogue.

The light that leads us out of that cave is the same light that guided our ancestors. It is the light of Faith, Family, and Freedom. It is the morality of a Christian society that teaches us to love our neighbor not by validating their delusions, but by speaking the Truth in love.

The erosion is advanced, but it is not irreversible. The foundation is cracked, but it is not gone. It is waiting for us to clear away the rubble of modernism, to pick up our tools, and to start rebuilding.

But we must choose. We can continue to drift downstream, tweeting our way into oblivion like Skyler, or we can plant our feet on the solid rock of our heritage and say: **"No further."**

The choice is ours. But as history tells us, the dark ages don't wait for permission to return. They just wait for the light to go out.

Let us keep the lamp lit.

www.ingramcontent.com/pod-product-compliance
Lightning Source LLC
LaVergne TN
LVHW090613110826
845146LV00001B/373

* 9 7 9 8 9 9 5 6 9 0 9 4 8 *